Switching Lanes
through Life

Switching Lanes
through Life

AKIL DORSEY SR.

authorHOUSE®

AuthorHouse™ LLC
1663 Liberty Drive
Bloomington, IN 47403
www.authorhouse.com
Phone: 1-800-839-8640

Published by AuthorHouse   09/17/2013

ISBN: 978-1-4918-1445-1 (sc)
ISBN: 978-1-4918-1444-4 (hc)
ISBN: 978-1-4918-1448-2 (e)

Library of Congress Control Number: 2013916347

Life doesn't begin until

A very precious life ends...

DEDICATIONS

I am dedicating this book to every child who lives in the ghetto· To every man, woman or child who is switching lanes through life and desperately trying to get it right for yourself, for your family and for the happiness of our GOD (ALLAH)·

I am dedicating this to you because in the midst of your struggle, you need to know that somebody does understand you and how hard it is to go through what you got to go through· Life ain't never been fair and I ain't sure if it'll ever get that way· Yet, I am sure that you gotta drive your car through traffic and sometimes you might be going fast or slow but you gotta switch lanes and keep it moving until you get it right·

I am dedicating this book to everyone who believes that they have the power to make their own situation better and only if they try harder than they ever have before· This is for you because you can do better, be better and if you strive hard enough, life will get better· This book is dedicated to all of my readers because a many of you can identify with parts of this story. Continue to make the best out of life and as you get lost in the pages understand that you ain't alone in your struggle for success. May GOD (ALLAH), continue to keep you focused. This story is for you.

ACKNOWLEDGEMENTS

ALLAH deserves the greatest acknowledgement of all. So many times I have come close to death and have put myself in uncompromising situations. Only through the grace of our GOD am I still alive and have been able to complete such a task as this. I am truly, truly grateful and beyond a doubt I know that I am blessed.

I must acknowledge all of my Haters! Yeah! There were plenty of you that believed I would stay down forever. Yet, I went through what I had to go through and I made it through the storm. I've grown so much mentally and I acknowledge that I was my worst enemy. I was the only one holding me back. Even though some of you, including a few family members, laughed at this project when I spoke of it, I want you to take your time and laugh now.

To everyone who helped get this off the ground, Thank You!!!!!!!!! If I start to name or acknowledge any of you, I may forget few and I damn sure don't want to do that. So, to everyone who was or is a part, you are being acknowledged and I appreciate you and the job that you have done.

PGB I acknowledge you 100% and Thank-You forever and forever you will be appreciated. You are not at the bottom; you'll always be a part of the top.

Nakita, you the best Honey and you've had my back since we were kids. Smile for me!!! This is nothing I ever dreamed of but it's real.

My children, my seeds, my life, I am sorry that I ran the streets and ran away from being a major part of your lives. Akil Jr., Ah'zia, Brittany, Akila, Elijah and Shaquan, I acknowledge you all existence. I am more than grateful for each of you and I really do believe in your futures. DO NOT FOLLOW IN MY FOOTSTEPS!!

I have made several mistakes throughout my life and I apologize because some of those selfish choices have kept me from being a full time father. Yet, I love each one of you and none, no more than the other because you are all my children and are equal. You are all so beautiful, smart, strong, and very much capable. Yes! You all are capable of becoming anything that you want to in this big bad world. Anything that you dream of you can do.

Always remember that I believe in you, I support you as your father in any positive endeavors you want to do in life. Be focused, be careful, be consistent and seek wisdom, so that you can make the correct choices in life. If you don't know write your father and ask me, I promise that if I don't know, I will try to find out, or we can figure it out together somehow. I definitely love you all and our blood is thick and the blood of A Bullet Proof Family. As I reach out to acknowledge you, don't any of you ever forget to acknowledge GOD (ALLAH), for all the blessings that he provides for you daily.

INTRODUCTION

A few blocks from the White House, around the corner from the United States Capitol building, drizzles of rain began lightly at first. The sounds of moving traffic could be heard on the wet pavement in the distance. As she walked across the parking lot, her thick ass hips bounced from side to side. Her movements were quick yet elegant. The rain had begun to stick to her pretty face. As her heels sloshed in and out of the puddles of water, she could've looked down at any time and seen her disheveled, brown skin, mirrored reflection bouncing back at herself.

She was tired, yet her brown eyes were open so wide and she was still rolling off the pills. She was frustrated, hurt and disgusted by the feeling of the warm semen that oozed from out of her and that began to slowly trickle down her thigh.

With desperation she weaved between several cars and trucks within the parking lot. As she searched for a certain vehicle, her Louis Vuitton satchel, bounced against one of her vivacious hips. It wasn't hardly enough to slow her down at all.

Then in an instant, her every move was cut completely short. She hadn't readied herself for death. She hadn't expected to meet her maker in the cold an in the rain. Nor did she dress for the occasion. It wasn't warm enough for a tight brown mini skirt. A low cut blouse, no stockings and a lot of cleavage.

With her hand on the hood of a Lincoln Navigator and one heel in the air, she made the attempt to turn by the truck. Yet four shots rang out simultaneously. She tumbled to the ground without a shoe on one foot and her short skirt rose just above her thighs. With barely any strength at all, she turned her head to look straight into the direction of the moon. Then as she moaned and struggled to allow air to enter her mouth, nose and lungs, a face appeared. Directly in front of the white glow of the moon, was the face of her killer.

She could see yet her vision was a total blur. She could see but she could not see clearly. A mouth was moving but her ears weren't working. She was confused, wounded and struggling for life. As she inhaled deeply and her sight faded in and out, she recognized it at once. What she saw was not a face; it was the barrel of the gun pointed directly down at her.

The first shot tore into her shoulder, rupturing her shoulder blade. The second shot missed and ricocheted off the pavement. The shooter fired two more shots into her midsection and her body jumped with each thud. Life was escaping her and the rain began to fall harder. She laid in the parking lot bleeding, the rain and her blood both mixed together and swam frantically for the nearest drain.

Thunder crackled loud and roared with intensity. Flashes of lightening shattered the sky line in the distance, piercing the night sky. Her killer bent over her and reached into her Louis Vuitton satchel and retrieved an iPad, hand held computer. Desperately the killer was hoping that they had found what they were looking for. The killer hit the power button and the screen blinked and the screen saver showed the image of a screen full of money. Then with a touch of the screen to activate its use, the water damage showed a pink and yellow line that ran from one corner of the screen to the very center. It turned into a terrible yet colorful mess.

As the killer was trying so hard to see if the iPad held whatever important information needed, the sounds of sirens began to scream even louder in the distance. With no time, no more life in the victim, the killer grabbed the bag off her shoulder and began to run. The killer began to run away from another situation. The killer tried to escape what might become a prosecution of death.

Chapter 1

Nine thirty p.m. and "Damn!" she hadn't showed. Only thirty minutes until lockdown and fifteen minutes more and visitation was over. I figured she wasn't coming and I was trying my best to hide my frustration. With such short time, I didn't want to look all pressed and shit. Little did I know, a rack of the fellas in the block had already peeped how far out of pocket I was.

On the way from my cell, I stopped and stared out of the big bay area window on the second floor. Scanning the parking lot, I searched for my baby's car. A cream colored Buick Regal Turbo that she adored. I saw a few people coming and going, so I even searched the crowd for her distinctive ass walk. None of those figures swayed the way she did. "Damn!" was all I could muster to say, as I headed for the shower.

The water wasn't anywhere near as hot as you would get it in your home. It sprayed out of the nozzle in a mist like form that felt Luke-warm by the time it hit your body. The tiles were covered with fungus and black mildew in some areas, mainly the

1

corners of the walls. Hairs of all colors littered the floor, along with shampoo bottles, soap wrappers, fruit flies, semen and whatever else that struggled to get down to the drain. Without the shower shoes on my feet, there is no telling what I might've latched onto my heels. My mind was clearly elsewhere. After I had washed and rinsed two good times. I just stood under the nozzle, letting the water fall down over my bald head thinking. Thinking about how this girl had my mind so far gone.

At the time, I was thirty-two and April was twenty-five and fine ass a muthafucka. I mean a beautiful black sista with a little bit of class and no damn direction. Not for a long time anyway. She would be on this one day and off following a new dream the next day.

The last time I had seen her was thirty days ago in the early part of November. April came to see me on a Friday night, right after she had gotten off of work. She bitched about the drive from New York Avenue in downtown Washington DC out to Upper Marlboro, Maryland but she came. A straight shot off of Central Avenue.

Before I had gotten into this situation, I would take her to work or pick her sexy ass up from that law firm she worked at. I never remembered the name because I actually never wanted to take the ride up to the seventeenth floor. Instead, I would wait in front of the beautiful building that sat across from the old Constitution Hall, on 10th and "H" Street, North West.

I would always smile when my sexy ass paralegal sashayed towards the car, with a laptop on her shoulder and a small briefcase in her hand. You could see the exhaustion on her face. Yet, she looked so spectacular in a pair of heels. They gave her ass a little added mmpphh. Which is just what the hell I said when she opened the visitation booth door that Friday.

Mmmpphh! Mmmpphh! Mmpphh!

April smiled and stood there in the doorway of the booth, letting me take it all in. Dark chocolate, no acne, cute face, shoulder length hair, that she let lay on her shoulders. April wore a teal green shirt that was squeezing her C-cups just right. Her black slacks hugged her hips as she stepped all the way into the booth. I smiled back after I looked down and noticed the black open toe sandals and the teal green polish on her pretty toes.

"Hey baby!" I gleamed as I grabbed the phone receiver and then watched her smile and grab the other phone.

"Hey Pooh!"

"Which is what she loved to call me for some damn reason, I never complained. If that is what she wanted me to be then that's what and who the hell I was for her any day. Pooh, Babe, Bay, all that then some.

"I spoke to your mom on the phone today while I was at work. She called and told me that she is feeling a lil better. It's hard to tell though Pooh. She still doesn't sound as vibrant. I'm supposed to go do her hair this weekend. She wants me to wash it and straighten it with a hot comb. Your momma is crazy boy, said she making some turkey neck bones and black eyed peas."

"Damn! I'm gonna miss all that good eating. Knowing momma she definitely gonna make some of that good ole, sweet, lumpy, bumpy, ass cornbread."

"I'm going and you better believe that."

"That's what's up," I said with a head gesture.

"Got my nails done, you like?"

"Yeah!" I responded as I watched April dangle her fingers in the air, showing off her well designed nails. I continued, "I've always told you that, that says a lot about how well a woman takes care of herself. Nice hands and nice feet mean a lot to a man. You

3

look cute and I like your nails baby. You are straight up doing the damn thing and I gotta say, I love that bluish green.

"You Gucci baby." I said with a smile.

"You a cold Bamma."

"Whatever."

"I just wanted to do something different to make you smile."

"You did that baby."

"Besides." She said as she got up batting her eyes. "The polish matches my panties."

My eyes opened wider and I could feel saliva building up in the corners of my mouth, so I swallowed hard. Then I watched April unbutton her pants and undo her belt. Swaying from side to side, she never took her brown eyes off me.

The visiting booth was secluded. He was in a small booth on the one side with a door leading out to a hallway. I was in the opposite booth and the only thing that separated us was glass. Which is exactly what I stared through as I watched my baby do what it do.

When April pulled those slacks down just below her thighs, I almost bit off my bottom lip. I could actually see directly through her boy shorts. It looked like she had a pad at the bottom of her pussy was sitting so fat. She kept that thing shaved bald as a beaver, just like I like it.

April took one hand and circled where her nipple was probably at. Using her index finger, she drew circles lightly on the fabric. Then she took the other hand and began to suck all on the other index finger. It fucked me up when she took it out of her mouth and let the saliva hang from her lip, as she pulled it away. Then quickly she sucked the spit back into her mouth.

I was overly excited and wishing that the glass wasn't in between us. I began rubbing my dick with long even strokes. It was hanging out of my jumpsuit

4

in plain view, just so that my baby could see every vein in it. April teased and I stroked. We made faces at one another and both of us panted and moaned through the phone receivers. It was hot! It was intense and it was our way of making love without ever touching one another.

Then as her hand began to trail down towards here shaved pussy, I stroked even faster. I just knew that she was gonna slide her fingers inside of her moist and warm box and let me watch. So, I worked faster and faster and stroked and stroked and.

"Mr. Deters! I know you heard me call lockdown!" The crazy ass C.O. yelled out as she stood in front of the half built shower door. She was looking me directly in my face. As her pretty, high yellow ass, stared at me she spoke again.

"Your nasty ass has got exactly two minutes to be in your cell or I'm writing your ass up."

"Got Damn!" You hot bitch!" I screamed out as my erection faded. "You just wanted to see the Loch Ness Monster, Ms. Wright. Looking all at my jewels."

"You better watch you muthafucking mouth that's for sure. I'm all my fifty years of living. I never thought I would come in contact with Tiny Tim. Now get your ass of that shower and lockdown," she said as she peeped down into the stall, before walking away.

I knew she meant business and the thing about it was Ms. Wright was pretty cool. I think we kept that sweet old lady young and in more ways than one, she shared with us her motherly advice sometimes. She was still on the opposite team but some of them folks are just working and don't take their jobs personal, those are the rare ones who'll help whenever it's possible.

In fact, I hurried to my cell, with my shower shoes squashing out water during each step. I had my towel and laundry bag in my hand and was moving quickly, when I looked up and noticed Ms. Wright waiting on the rail by my door. She was actually leaning over it, watching the T.V. that swiveled in the corner of the tier. Ain't no way she didn't know half of the block was in their doors, watching her every move. I believe she knew and that attention is what prompted her to wear the bright red lipstick that complemented her yellow skin so well. She damn sure managed to keep herself in excellent, excellent shape over the years. With her hair done in so many different styles and as often as it was, many said that it was the work of her daughter. A freckle faced young sista who resembled her mother with a very strong likeness. When I passed by Ms. Wright leaning over the rail, I glanced over at her vivacious curves. They were definitely built alike.

I entered my cell and looked back over my shoulder, "Thank-You."

But she didn't accept that so well. Instead of immediately shutting the door and locking it, she stepped inside of the doorway and let it rest against her back and hip.

"Listen Honey. I could have been a bitch about things but you never give me any trouble around here."

As she spoke, I placed a towel on the floor and stepped on it barefoot. Then with a bottle of baby oil, I began to put the oil in one of my hands, and rubbed them together repeatedly.

"Now respect me enough to make it to your cell on time young man. How about doing that for me please?"

After rubbing the oil into my palms real good, I slapped the oil on my chest shoulders, and arms. I was glistening like a well-lit Christmas tree. Or a bright ass star. Before I responded to that comment I noticed her eyes move up and down my body."

"Yes mam."

"Tomorrow when I come in, you're gonna clean those showers for me, Spider."

"Damn! What made you call me that?" I asked with a puzzled ass look.

"Honey you've got spiders tattooed all over your body. Ooh! Two of them on your feet. Now, I know I've seen it all. You just be prepared to do showers for me Spider man because I will be here tomorrow."

Ms. Wright smiled and turned out the doorway, leaving me in the cell slapping baby oil everywhere. I couldn't do anything but smirk because I loved the attention her sweet smelling, old ass, gave me. The key turned in the lock and I prepared myself for some much needed rest with hopes of seeing the next day.

Getting to sleep isn't always an easy thing to do when you're laced up in a jail cell, staring up at the walls. Sometimes your mind does plenty of traveling, having you think about your past, present, and future. Just heavy in thought about what all moves need to be made when it's all over with. The exact ways a man could repair his life and make every move count.

I drifted off to sleep thinking about April and why the hell she hadn't come to see me. That last time was definitely special but there wasn't any time like the present. I had all the intentions of calling her the next day.

Chapter 2

I got up the following morning right before the sun popped up and slid down out of my rack. I immediately hit the floor and prostrated with the intentions of giving much thanks for my blessings in spite of my whereabouts. Usually I hop back in the bed for a lil more sleep. This particular morning, I tied my shank to my inner thigh like I always did. Every man needs to be prepared and I was always better off with mine than without it. I sat on my rack, drank a few cups of that nasty ass tap water and then read. The book was titled, *Foundations of the Sunnah*, by Imam Ahmad Hanbal.

When the key turned, I went out into the day room and fixed myself a piping hot cup of coffee. After taking a few sips, I glanced up at the news and realized it was supposed to be a beautiful day. Without being able to contain myself any longer, I headed for the death trap. Yes! That's right, the death trap. It'll damn sure cause some things to happen. Either you killing somebody, somebody killing you, or you getting so far gone over it, that you get weak and kill your damn self.

"Good morning Mr. Bracey," I said to an older gentleman in his early sixties with a low wavy haircut.

"I'm fine thank-you."

"The phones aren't on yet. They should be on in a few. I see you've fixed yourself a cup of that Joe."

"I've got a lil extra, if you like, I can run to my room and grab you a shot of that, a shot of creamer, and a few sweeteners."

"No don't trouble yourself."

"I suggest," I insisted.

"Well, I'll tell you what young man. Since you suggest, just sit yourself down on over here with an old fella and pour me a sip or two of what you got in that big ole mug of yours. That should do me quite fine, I reckon."

"Alright," I responded as I sat down next to him in a blue chair under the phone.

I leaned over and grabbed Mr. Bracey's coffee stained mug. You could tell he was a true coffee drinker. The mug had looked like it hadn't been washed since he had it. Yet, he was at a point in his bit where he couldn't afford to go to commissary. I damn sure had been there, so why the hell not help out the next man. Never know when I might be in need. When I poured the older fella what I had, you could see the steam rising from both of our cups. The rich aroma of coffee filled the cell block, covering the stale smell of what once lingered.

"I've gotta call the Mrs."

"I can dig it Mr. Bracey. I'm trying to do the same thing. Check on my lady friend."

"Well, if you don't mind I wanna ask you something Son."

"Yeah! Go ahead." I said as I leaned in a little.

"Did you hear all that ruckus this morning?"

"No! I have no idea what you are talking about. What ruckus?"

With the wire rim Versace glasses on the tip of his nose, he looked at me puzzled. Then after he took a sip of his coffee, he told me in a voice close to a whisper.

"Around about 4:00 a.m. or so, about six officers were down here on the first floor. Right over there by the rec door. I could not figure it out at first, what type of shit they were doing. You know from where my cell is up there in the corner, it makes it pretty rough to see."

"Yeah! Go ahead."

"Well, I saw two of them running back a lil bit, away from the rest. I mean trying to get away. Then the crazy thing was, I saw Ms. Clarke run her sexy ass to the office and get a big bag. You should've seen that sista."

"What happened?" I asked with curiosity.

"She was looking like a beautiful black stallion, galloping across the block."

"What the hell were they doing?"

"I finally saw all of them run in the opposite corner with a box."

"That big ass box that the toilet paper comes in?"

"Right."

"They got it! Yeah! They got the lil sucka that's for sure. Trapped him in that box with the broom. Then they let the lil sucka go out the rec. door this morning about a lil after 5:00 a.m."

"What the hell was it?" I demanded.

"A black bird."

"Man you've been going on and on about a black bird? Wow! I thought it was something serious. You faking like shit. I'm jive fucked up with you about this one."

"Look here· Don't be so loud," said Mr· Bracey after looking around to see if anyone had been listening· Satisfied, he continued, "Son, if you didn't know, black birds mean DEATH! Yeah! That's right, they mean DEATH·

"I'm not superstitious Mr· Bracey·" I'm not either· Yet I know from prior experience that when a back bird flies into your home, death is sure to follow· I know because it happened when I was sixteen and my sister was pregnant· A bird flew in our home and I got a broom· Me, my mother, and my sister shooed it out of my lil sister's bedroom window and yeah·"

"Yeah what?"

"My lil sister's baby died right after birth· Fucked everybody up· My grandmother told us about the bird but nobody believed her· The baby was born but got lucky enough to leave this old fucked up ass world, just as fast as he came in it· He lived for one day, twenty three hours, six minutes, and twelve seconds·"

"Damn! So, what the hell does that mean besides death? Who the hell is about to die?"

"I can't tell you that· Just remember that I did tell you· So, guard your own soul and make sure your right with the Creator, just in case he is coming to get you·"

"Yeah alright," I said in disbelief· "Maybe your right·"

"Look here," said Mr· Bracey in an irritated tone· "If there is one thing I know, it's death· I've been locked up now nineteen years cuz these people say that I killed a muthafucka in the Marshall Heights area way back in the day· A cold blooded murder committed by a bunch of wild ass teens one night· I am innocent and although I saw the blood running down the sidewalk and body of the victims laying on the basketball court in Eastgate· I am innocent· I just happened to witness a senseless murder and the worse part of it was exactly who the hell got murdered that night. Yet, some people deserve to die and others are killed for no damn reason at all. I have been watching good men die inside this system. Die over a channel on a TV over where they're from. Die over their race or simply because they were to uneducated to stay alive. I know about death and I know you better guard your own soul son because its coming."

"Yeah alright!" I said reluctantly.

"I'll hollar at you later. I've got to go take my insulin shot before breakfast. Guess I'll have to call the Mrs. a lil later."

Mr. Bracey walked off and left me sitting there looking some kind of crazy in the face. My coffee was cold and I wasn't about to spend my damn morning trying to figure out who the hell was about to die. For all I knew, it could've been his fly, old ass or he might've been about to put the work in on somebody else for all I knew. The last swallow of the coffee went down quick and afterwards I wiped off the phone and dialed up April's number. I listened to the long automated procedure to put the call through; I figured it to be crazy when I heard the recording say the number had been disconnected. So, I dialed her up again, believing that I had dialed the wrong number.

Chapter 3

I had just spoken to April about four days prior over the phone. We kicked it about the hell of a good time we had at the Six Flags amusement park in Largo, Maryland. It was a spot that everybody in and around the Metropolitan area visited at least once. A lot of kids from the D·M·V· worked there on Saturdays and Sundays, the park was off the chain. April looked great the last time we went there. She looked like a million bucks in a two piece bathing suit then and I was messed up I wasn't seeing her now.

I got the same message. So, I hung up and called her ass again, while I tried to remember what else we had discussed. Nothing major came to mind and with disgust, I went through the phone's procedures again. April had explained how she was intending to sign up for a few classes at U·D·C· (The University of the District of Columbia), yet that had clearly nothing to do with why I sat there listening to the recording say that the number was disconnected for the fifth time.

The phone was in my name. April's credit was shot to hell behind her being a part of a check scamming scheme. The Feds were forcing her to pay back fines and restitution for the $830,000 worth of checks she had cashed. Out of three involved, she caught the light end of the deal and got three years and a shit load of probation. The peoples were on her back so hard she was against buying anything or putting anything in her name. So, I helped her with the phone account. I spent most of my time with her so it wasn't nothing. I would be using the damn thing too.

April and I met right after she had finished her sentence for the Feds. It was rather coincidental, that I had just finished a four and a half year sentence for the state of Virginia my damn self, for an armed robbery. I was convicted after a witness testified that I followed and robbed three niggas in the parking lot of the Pentagon City Mall. We were like two peas in the pod. My sister-in-law Alecia introduced us as two jail birds over the phone. Told me she had a friend fresh out of jail who she thought I would love to meet.

Never before had I dated a woman who had went so hard. April was from uptown, 14th and Clifton in Washington, DC and she overly expressed it. She was a true fan of the Backyard band and tried to never miss a good Go Go, where BYB was featured. I would argue with her that Junkyard band or otherwise known as, The Good JY was better but she would protest so hard. April would get up and sing out of Backyard's cuts, while dancing all around in excitement, with her hands in the air, titties bouncing and ass shaking.

"Fuck the Bamma's!" She would sing out.

"Fuck the Bamma's!"

Sentenced to three years in the Feds and with $20,000 she managed to beat an accessory to murder in the state of Maryland. Many say she was the driver of a car believed to be seen fleeing from a homicide. Let her tell it, she just had a similar car to the one described. A white 1998 Mazda Millennium that she whipped around in. Others say, a car pulled up behind

14

a baller named Peanut early one morning, caught him loafing, putting bags in his trunk. The young niggas wasted no time. They shot Peanut twice in the back of his head, took the bags out and put him in the trunk. Two of them drove off in his 2010; grey 750 IL BMW and one supposedly jumped back in the car with April. He was found dead two days before her trial in a field on Walker Mill Road in Maryland. His lips had been cut off his face and a substance believed to be a powder acid was also found on his face, yet it wasn't applied properly. If it had've been enough or even applied with water it would have left him totally unrecognizable, instead of just without a set of lips. The second shot to the head was the kill shot that left him deceased. Without a doubt he had been tortured and his death was meant to set an example.

With all that behind her, April got out on house arrest and after we had spoken on the phone so much in the beginning, I started keeping her company. I would head over to Hyattsville, Maryland on the Metro train. Which managed to be an hour ride away and a transfer from the blue line to the green line.

April was at her moms and I had taken refuge in my father's basement on Aster Place in South East, DC. My dad would take me to the Benning Road station, thinking I was on my way to look for a job. I'd spend the day with my baby, laid up watching videos, fucking, licking and sucking on each other. We would make out in every damn area of her momma's small ass apartment. From the living room, to the kitchen counter, in either bedroom and on to some water games, where we would be fucking and funning in the shower. Other times we would sit and soak in the tub until our toes were wrinkled.

Playing in her momma's house eventually got old. We both needed some money and we weren't gonna get it laid up in an apartment in the Cypress Creek complex. After I had got caught coming up out of there one evening, we both decided to step the game up.

Chapter 4

I brought some newspapers and a focused mind. April set the phone on the table and left me to get on her mother's computer. She typed and browsed all over the internet, even conformed herself a well written resume. I called several contractors and tried to find myself a good job in the construction field.

From absolutely nothing, me and April worked to make something out of our lives again. The job of repair wasn't easy and what kept us believing that we could, was each other. April encouraged me and kissed me. I encouraged her and fucked her young sexy ass like my mind was gone bad. All that sneaking and freaking during the day time eventually paid off for the both of us. I found a job and so did April.

During the time I spent incarcerated in the Virginia system I gained a certificate as a Plumbers Helper. Yet just how much I knew about the Plumbing field was questionable indeed. None the less, my baby found a local Plumbers Union in the Maryland area by browsing the web. So, I went down to sign up.

The Union accepted my application immediately and gave me a three page list of contractors. Not to mention, a list of union dues and the address of the school I would be attending twice a week. An apprenticeship course that would likely open up the doors to a better future for the both of us. All I had to do was find a contractor who would be willing to let me work.

Phillip Smoot was his name; he was listed under Diamond Cutz Construction. A business that had been up and running for eleven years. I called and after a sexy sounding secretary put me on hold, for what seemed like forever, Mr. Smoot finally jumped on the phone.

"This is Mr. Smoot with Diamond Cutz, the construction that will last forever. A man's best friend. How can I help you?"

"Mr. Smoot, my name is Asim Deters and I recently signed up at the Local #5. I've been given a list to find one who'll be willing to accept me as a worker. I am focused, willing individual, determined and . . ."

"Wait a minute son, slow down."

"Yes sir." I said as I was cut off abruptly.

"Are you an apprentice?" he asked.

"I'm a certified plumber's helper and I've received 144 hours of hands on experience and text book work."

"Do you have transportation?"

"Yes sir," I lied.

"Well, listen here Mr. Deters. The whole eleven years I've worked I've never given out a job over the phone. This industry is a very hard one. Built for hard working individuals who are serious about what they do. Your best bet at finding a job is to get out in the field young man. A boss can't see a potential good worker through a phone call. Don't even know if you're willing to get downright dirty for the money."

"I definitely am Sir."

"Well son, the only way to dig trenches big enough for a sewage pipe line is to get down in them, and dig. Good luck to ya and hopefully you'll find what you're looking for Mr. Deters."

"Thank-you sir," I said reluctantly.

"You're welcome son goodbye."

Somehow not hearing what you want to hear can ruin your spirits. After so many No's you look forward to a Yes sooner or later. I didn't get one, but I be damned if I let that stop me. I made it to the office and it was located way out in another area of Maryland, called Burtonsville. Once I got there, I was asked to have a seat.

Ms. Babet left me in the waiting area which was actually just two chairs on the other side of her desk. She stepped out front while we waited for Mr. Smoot. Ms. Babet decided to have herself a cigarette. While she was outside, I stood up to stretch. With a huge yawn and my arms open wide, I noticed a small safe with a Louis Vuitton handbag sitting on top with gold buttons.

Ms. Babet was a dark skin, slim sista with hair extensions that went just past her ears. She didn't have those luscious ass curves that every man desires. She was average but had a radiant smile, an even brown skin tone and a set of titties that left me staring all down at her cleavage before she left out to smoke. She was wearing a peach and brown, pants suit and a pair of brown heels to match.

While she ignored the Surgeon General warning, I stretched and noticed that small safe behind her desk sat ajar. So, with a quick glance, I could see Ms. Babet gossiping through the tinted glass on her cell phone. The only thing she was able to notice was her own mirrored reflection from the outside, as she talked and talked and talked some more.

Like a large cat, I crouched down and around the desk with agile speed. When I opened the safe, the rest of the way, stacks of money and neatly stacked papers filled the safe and were in clear view· So, with no time to count, I reached in and grabbed six large stacks that were wrapped in paper bands· Abruptly I stood up and stuffed the money in various pockets, then just as I was getting ready to go back for a seventh or more, I heard the front door open· So, with my leg, I pushed the safe closed and stepped over several feet to the coffee machine·

Immediately, I began pouring a cup· Ms· Babet turned sideways and she slid by me to get to her desk, I could smell the strong mixed aroma of perfume, cigarettes and coffee·

"Excuse me honey·"

"Oh sure," I said with a smile·

Then as I went to my seat, Ms· Babet slid down in hers and looked up at me so seductively· I avoided her teasing advances and went on through with the interview and the walk through of the warehouse· I managed to get the job and even kept it for a short period of time· While there, April was proud of me for grinding like a square· With the $30,000 I eased into our lives as smooth as butter· Life definitely got better for us both, not knowing our past; it became extremely hard for anyone to tell we were two convicted felons in love·

For April's 26ᵗʰ birthday, I bought her that cream colored 2012 Buick Regal Turbo that she was driving· Knowing she loved to chauffeur her nephew Nookie around so much, I got two TVs installed in the back of each front seat head rest· The monitor in the dash wasn't enough· Lil Nookie could enjoy every DVD made for the enjoyment of an eight year old, while riding in style·

Our relationship got so heated that we decided to share our living expenses totally· My credit wasn't the exact greatest, yet it allowed us to grab a nice two bedroom condo in the Maryland area· It was small and it sat in a high rise on Brinkley Road, near the Rosecroft Race Track, overlooking a park.

I worked for Mr. Smoot and while I was doing so, April was downtown on the other end. In fact, I was not too far from the World Bank, at 22nd and K Street, North West, in DC. On my lunch breaks, I would sit on the roof and stare down at the heavily guarded building. There were armed security personnel at every entrance and all over the three blocks that the building occupied. A sting like that would be in the millions and well worth planning for. It would be the hardest job to ever accomplish. After it was over, there wouldn't be any need to ever break the law again. I'd have enough money to set me straight forever, or so I thought anyway.

Chapter 5

I had to figure out how the hell I was gonna get out of jail. I had been offered a plea agreement for twenty years, for the attempted murder that I was being held on. Without a doubt, I had declined such an offer and damn sure wasn't interested in the next one that the prosecution team had to offer me.

My lawyer was a sharp ass dressing Italian named Velario Elegany. He was mid-forties, stocky with a huge belly from eating all the damn pasta. Rumors had it that he was heavily respected in the court room. I was destined to see. Everybody was so set on me getting found guilty but I couldn't figure out how the hell that was gonna happen. Prosecution had no gun, one flaky ass witness and the victim got hit seven times in a dark ass alley. So what, I had on clothes, matching the same description as the shooter. Every nigga wears black at night and North Face is worn by any and everybody throughout the D.M.V.

I wandered around the block contemplating on exactly how I would spend my day. The phone was disconnected and I just couldn't figure it out. Even though the bill was in my name, it didn't make any sense· The television was never enough to hold me· I hated board games, all except chess· Which had always been explained to me as a thinking man's game· After standing over two young cats, watching them play, it didn't take long to see that neither one of them had the answer·

I spotted Mr· Bracey sitting by the bay area window eating an orange· I figured I would give the old guy some company and I headed to my cell to grab my chair· As soon as I got in good, I heard·

"Mr· Deters, you're wanted in the Lieutenant's office· I know you're in there Mr· Deters·"

With a stare of disbelief, I looked at the silver box on the wall· Then with disgust, I yelled back·

"Yeah! Alright, DAMN! I heard you and I'll be down there SHIT!"

"Make sure you have on your jumpsuit·"

I hadn't any idea what the hell I was being called for· I had figured it to be about the grievance form that I had filled out, on how cold the food was by the time it hit the block· I got dressed and looked in the dull grey make shift mirror on my wall· Seeing the vague image of myself, after I slapped on a little cocoa butter lotion, I figured I was ready· You never know who the hell you might see in the halls·

I was escorted from the back section of the Upper Marlboro Jail and we walked through several hallways to get to the Lieutenant's office· I saw a few female CO's that I knew who spoke and made me grin like a chest cat· I got a wink from the boxing coach D and I knew he really wanted to ask me why the hell I hadn't come to the gym, the previous week·

All throughout the hall, the sun was extremely bright and it glared off the hallway floors· I noticed how nice it looked outside, when we passed the smoking area windows· Then a sharp ass pain shot through my chest and went all the way down to my feet· A pain that I could never explain, yet it faded just as the CO led me into an office.

"Mr. Deters," said the Lieutenant, as he stood on the opposite side of the only desk in the room. Seated next to him was a dark skin man who I almost didn't recognize.

"Yes! Mr. Deters I am Chaplain Obejawue and it's important that we have you here."

"Yeah! I know who you both are. What's going on? What's good?" I asked while looking down at a small yellow tablet on the desktop. Immediately I spotted my little sister's name and a strange phone number.'

Niki Deters (202) 555-1242

"Oh hell nah!" I screamed.

"I'm terribly sorry Mr. Deters but you need to place a call to your family sir. Your sister has called and informed us of some very tragic news. I am gonna allow you some time to contact your family to be more aware of the details sir."

"Mr. Deters me and the Chaplain are gonna step out to respect your privacy Sir. We are definitely sorry to hear about your troubles."

After putting the call through, they both walked out of the office. I forced myself to grab the receiver. As I listened to the phone ring on the opposite end, I watched the Chaplain thumb through a Bible on the other side of the doorway.

"Hello," said a very weak female voice.

"Hello."

"Oh Asim! Oh my GOD. NO! NO! NOOOO!!!"

"I'm here, what is it baby girl?"

"It's momma! Oh it's momma! I can't. Oh! No!" Niki said as she wailed into the phone and sobbed uncontrollably.

A tear ran out of one of my eyes as I listened to my baby sister cry hard. Her screams were loud and they went on and on. Then those screams faded along with her unclear words. Every inch of her pain was my pain and I felt it in the pit of my stomach, the center of my heart and on down to the soles of my feet.

"Asim this is your Aunt Piggy and it's your mother baby."

"What happened?"

"Well, your mother is right here and it's so bad. She is in a coma. The doctors have her on a breathing machine that is providing oxygen for her. I'm afraid it's very serious Asim. Oh my sister! Oh God No!"

"Damn!" was all I could muster to say.

I looked at the Chaplain and he was into a scripture, reading away with all seriousness. As I tried to strain to see exactly where he was reading from, I heard rattling on the opposite end of the phone line.

"Asim this here is your Uncle Joe. Your momma is about to go boy. I'm here with Aunt Piggy, Aunt Michelle and Uncle Jeff. It's the worse I ever seen my big sister. We praying and Ahh man, we just praying. Talk back to your sister and pray boy pray."

"Asim, you there?"

"Yeah! I'm here and Damn! Is it that bad Niki?"

"Yes! She can't even breathe for herself. Oh, I'm so scared."

"Listen! You've gotta be strong. Damn it! I'm not there. Take her place, she gonna be alright. I know she gonna be OK."

"Momma wrote it in her Will, that she was not to be left on any life support machines."

"I'm sorry Mr. Deters but we have to get you back to the block. It's count time sir." Said the Lieutenant as he leaned in the doorway.

"Don't you let them bastards take my momma off that damn machine!" I yelled into the phone.

"I'm not," said Niki. "I'm here with her, I ain't leaving her side. I will sleep in this muthafucka right next to her. I promise."

"OK look," I said as I tried so very hard to contain feelings of rage, grief and misunderstanding.

"Mr. Deters we gotta take you back sir." Said the Chaplain as he laid the Bible on the desk in front of me.

"What the fuck · · · ·"

"Oh! No Asim. Stop!" Niki screamed into the phone, cutting me off.

"Man yall hold the fuck up!" I mentioned with anger. "This is my muthafucking mother! I'll take on the whole damn goon squad. Damn it!"

"Asim stop! Just do like they say. I don't need you in the hole. Stop! The family is going through enough. Stop! Please just stop!"

"OK. Babygirl." I responded reluctantly.

"Mr. Deters we are so sorry sir, but if you fill out a request form, you will be likely awarded a new phone call in about a week or so, with Chaplain Obejawue. Please, Mr. Deters disconnect your call." The Lieutenant said, then walked back towards the doorway and kept his back towards us.

I couldn't contain the tears and several fell down each side of my face. I could feel so much hurt, resentment, anger and even a lil shame. It was all so deep. I swallowed hard.

"Niki, I love you baby girl. Kiss momma for me."

"I will. I love you too and try to call back here tonight if they let you. I will leave the phone lines open just for your call. Oh yeah! Asim · · ·"

"Yeah!"

"Don't do anything stupid."

"OK bye"

"Bye."

After I hung up the phone, I walked down the hallway and I never felt my feet hit the ground. I don't even remember really and I don't recall anything other than seeing my momma face, flash through my head so many times. My pain was unbearable. This was momma and you only get one. There isn't a person on this earth that's gonna love you like she do. In her eyes, I could do no wrong and she always had my back. Caught with a gun and standing directly over top a still warm body, momma would've said, "My baby ain't do that."

I was crushed and in a slump like no other. I couldn't eat. I wouldn't eat and I felt like I couldn't or wouldn't sleep. Whenever my senses came back around, I was sitting on the floor under my window.

At that time, I prided myself on being a gangsta but there are a few reasons that a man's spirit can actually be broken. This had indeed been one of those rare moments. I decided to take a nap during the count time, hoping that it would help to clear my head.

When I woke up, I didn't feel any better and the pain seemed to get so much deeper. I stepped outside in the rec. area and watched a real decent handball game with a dude named Snap and Shane. Shane bragged about how nice he was and on this evening. Snap tore into his ass some kind of special. Gave the Homey everything he was looking for. Shane challenged him to a rematch and Snap declined that politely. Hands down, Snap was D-best and he let you know it if you jumped out there with him. He would play anybody and his record proved that he could damn near beat everybody.

I enjoyed the match and the joint of bush ass weed, could've been better, the two necks of mash made me feel somewhat better. I walked back in and grabbed the last phone and bounced down on the blue chair. I scanned my surroundings, wiped off the receiver with my t-shirt, then blew into the phone a few times and placed my call.

"Hey Pop"

"As Salaam Alaikum son. How are you holding up in there? Is everything alright with you?"

"No!"

"What's wrong son?"

"My mother is in the hospital and they are saying that she might not make it. Damn! I don't know what to do."

"Wow! Your mother's daughter, I mean, your sister called two days ago but she just said that your mother was sick and taking a very strong medication for some pain. I think it was Morpohol or Morphine. Something like that. Your sister said your mother was having a lil trouble with her liver. Damn! Is it that bad now?"

"It's bad. Man it's real bad. I don't know. I am just . . ."

"You need to slow down. I want you to slow down Asim. I'm gonna call on the three way, so we can both see what the hell is going on. Will it hang up if I call?"

"No! I'll blow in the phone. When you click over and place the call, don't click back over to me, until somebody answers."

"Go! Wheeewwww!!!"

"Click!"

I listened to the silence for a few seconds hoping that Niki would answer and our call wouldn't be disconnected. My baby sister had plenty of features like momma, yet she resembled Keisha Knight Pulliam, somewhat. Niki and momma would be pressing each other's hair and shopping together for all sorts of clothes and shoes. Whenever you saw one, you saw the other. They were inseparable.

"Hello I'm here," Niki whispered into the phone.

"Son."

"Yeah! I'm here Pop."

"Niki," said my father. "I'm here yall."

After I was satisfied that we were all on the line, I questioned, "Babygirl, what's going on? Where is Ma?"

"She right here and so is Aunt Piggy. Momma's lips are cracked and so dry. Aunt Piggy used a sponge to give momma some water. Just like the lady did Jesus, with the wine on the hyssop." Then she said in a much softer tone "Talk to her. I'm gonna give her the phone."

I could hear the loud noises of the machine that they were using to help my mother breathe with. She never uttered a word an I just listened.

My father intervened, "Say something to your mother, son."

Yet, there were so many tears welling up in the souls of my eyes that I didn't know what the hell to say, without bursting into a terrible crying rendition. For a minute, I just sat there in silence and in total disbelief. Then beyond reasons I even know, I began to sing momma's favorite song. The one song that we would sing together sometimes.

"Amazing grace, how sweet the sound · · ·"

My voice trembled and although I tried to prevent the tears from falling, they flowed all the way down my face, one after another. I can't remember seeing anyone and if they had've noticed, there is no doubt that it was more than obvious that what I was going through, at that moment, was incredibly serious. Then suddenly Niki screamed into the phone.

"She moved!!! She moved!!! Asim, momma moved. Oh my GOD!!! She heard your voice and she moved. She really squeezed my finger."

"That's beautiful Niki," said my father. "It means she could hear him," he coached into the phone. "It's gonna be OK she's strong. She'll pull through."

"I've got about two minutes left yall." I said while now feeling a little more at ease."

"OK Asim, I love you and good luck tomorrow in court," Niki said with a slight clearer voice.

"Son, call me and As Salaam Alaikum."

"Wa laikum As Salaam and I love yall both dearly, goodbye."

Chapter 6

Later on that night, after the cell doors were locked and it was quiet, I had managed to find my way on the floor under my window again. It had become my spot to sit and think and with two chairs in the cell, I can't even say why I chose the floor of all places.

My cell buddy hadn't said much of one word to me and truthfully, I believe it was because he knew that not much could be said. As I came out of thought, I noticed a tall cup of what looked like water sitting beside me. Plenty of people disliked my cell buddy and there were so many reasons why. He had a natural tendency to say whatever the hell he was feeling and about any damn thing at all. He would wear his jail jumpsuit, unbuttoned and sometimes dingy as hell. His dreads looked greyish, yet brown and to put it plain and simple, he just didn't give a damn; neither about his appearance or the words that came out of his mouth. Yet in spite of all the fights and stabbing altercations this young wild ass dude had been into, there was clearly another side to him that I only knew.

"Hey Slim! I'm real sorry about your mom's man. I already know that there isn't much at all I could ever say to ease your pain. I do want you to know that your my Big Homey, Slim. I fucks with you too hard. Take a sip from that cup and get your ass up off that floor."

"Say what?"

"You heard me, get up off that floor and get yourself together nigga. I got two fat ass jays of some purp that Lil Mike gave me before lockdown. He was fucked up about everything and he sent his condolences."

"Oh yeah!" I said, as I stood and stretched, with the cup now in my left hand.

Slob passed me the jay and I took three totes, instead of the usual two and pass. My mouth was damn sure dry as hell from having been sitting for so long. Yet, when I took a sip, I damn near choked.

"Yeah!" Slob said while smiling. "That's that White Lighting nigga."

"Damn!" I said with shock, and then wiped my mouth, with the back of my hand.

"That's just what it felt like going down." I continued. "That had to be the first pull."

"I believe so. Fuck what pull it was. You need to pull that bitch April's heart right out of her muthafucking chest."

"Go ahead with that shit."

"Look one thing for certain Spider. She lied and not just to you but to your mother. She was supposed to go get her and do her hair right?"

"Yeah!" I responded.

"Pass me that drink. Hell, if that's the case you would've gotten a chance to see her before she got sick. Then to top it all off, she ain't show up yesterday."

"I've been thinking about all that and then some believe me. Can you fade this?" I asked as I handed him the roach.

"You know I can nigga."

"I've got court in the morning and man; this is a whole lot of shit, for real."

"That's why we getting fucked up, so you can think a little better," said Slob with a chuckle.

"You funny as shit but I ain't got the strength to laugh."

"How about you tell me what the hell you're gonna do if you get lucky enough to beat this bullshit ass case they got you on? Tell me to help you, so I can call around Edgewood and get a few of my muthafucking men, to snatch her up. Then duct tape her chocolate ass to a chair. Yeah! But with her ass up in the air, then after they take turn fucking her all up in her ass they can · · ·"

"Nigga I thought you was a killer. Now you a butt bandit? Fire up that other jay nigga."

"Fool I just got sentenced to 180 months; I ain't never going in a nigga ass. In spite of all the rumors we get about us coming out of Washington, you better believe that there are some real men who can do a bid without breaking for that bullshit. Ain't you one of them?"

"That's a question that needs not answering lil nigga. The only rumor that will carry any weight is me getting money, and pushing a piece of steel if a nigga violate."

"That's what the hell I'm talking about. Now your simple ass, still need to duct tape that bitch. I don't know what the hell made you get a joint account with her and especially after you done stacked all that paper. That makes you so damn stupid. You like a nigga that take a GED test but can't spell or tell what the hell GED means."

"Man go ahead. That's why, you open your mouth and it look like the back of the bus. Like you inhaled all that black ass smoke and it done stained your crooked ass teeth."

31

Those last few hours of the night, went by pretty fast. Slob did everything he could to comfort me and keep me from breaking down. We both fell asleep for what little bit of time we could. Then just that quick, the cell doors were being opened for me to go to court.

Chapter 7

After making it over to the courthouse, the cells were cold, jam packed and everybody was trying to stay warm and comfortable on a concrete floor. I had laid on my side for so long that my hip had gotten sore, so I shifted to the other. Then I took off my boots and lay on them as if I had a pillow. Nothing worked for too long. The sounds of the toilet, not too many feet away would wake anybody up out a dream.

When the Sheriff came to open the cell door, I thought that it was just to bring us those cold as bologna and cheese sandwiches and milks.

"Mr. Deters, your attorney wants to see you."

I got up and looked around at the few other restless inmates who were eagerly awaiting their prize moments. I was handcuffed and taken to the Attorney/Client room.

"Hey kid! Have a seat."

"Thanks! What's going on Mr. Elegany? How are things looking?"

"Well, honestly, things are looking pretty good on this case in P.G. County. Although you've been accused of shooting a man 7 times and the lead Detective, Adam Woods, wants you bad. It's looking good on that end."

"I already told you I ain't shoot nobody and their evidence is beyond weak."

"Look kid! I don't give a fuck if you did shoot the bastard. My job is to get you off, that's it, plain and simple. Those attempted murder charges are being dropped, you lucky son of a bitch."

"What? Who the fuck you talking to like that?"

"Look! Sorry I blew a fucking haystack with you kid. Shit is very complicated. The prosecutor agreed to drop those charges because she knew she didn't have a strong enough case. Either that or they weren't able to convince the witness to come to court on you."

"Yeah! That's what the fuck I'm talking about P.G. County is sweet as a muthafucka."

When I stood up and began to express a little excitement, Mr. Elegany motioned for me to sit back down with his hand. If we had not been separated through the glass, I would've reached out and hugged the man. Yet he wasn't finished.

"Kid, that's the good news. The bad news is that when you got arrested on this, the arresting officer, Peter Lamond, claimed he found a loaded .40 caliber, semi-automatic, under the driver's seat."

"What?" I questioned with shock.

Mr. Elegany looked down at a piece of paper in his manila folder and asked, "Do you or did you ever possess a gun with the serial number 0070370837? Have you ever purchased a weapon in your name?"

"Nah! Nah! To both of them questions. How is it that they coming with this shit all of a sudden?"

"Technically they can because the statute of limitations damn sure hasn't expired. Besides that, the car is in your name. I've got some pictures in my office and I'll bring them with me when I visit you at that Upper Marlboro Jail again. It's a beautiful, baby blue, 1974 Coupe de Ville, with white leather interior· I owned one myself way back in the day· You've got class kid," he said with a smile, trying to make light of the situation·

"Yeah! That's my caddy but it damn sure ain't my gun·"

"I understand· Listen! You're gonna be placed under the custody of the Feds· They will be responsible of handling your case· Unfortunately I can't represent you because I have only taken the bar exam for Ohio and Maryland· You will be appointed a federal public defender, whom should take good care of you, Mr· Deters·"

"Can you set it up for me to handle the detainer they have on me for the City of Virginia?"

"I will take care of that a·s·a·p· Would you happen to have heard anything about the shooting of a young black female over a designer bag? It has been all over the news· The press is making it a very large case·"

"What?"

"I'm sorry to be asking but you or anybody else's cooperation would prove to be real worthy to the D·A· Apparently they want the actual perpetrator real bad·"

"Man I ain't no fucking snitch and I damn sure don't know anything about no bitches getting robbed over no funky ass pocket books·"

Chapter 8

Somehow things happened all so fast in between that next week. My mother surely passed and I felt like my own soul had drifted up out of me, after I had gotten the news. I had sensed it and now that it did happened, there were so many other issues lying ahead of me. My family prepared her burial; I was still desperately trying to find April. Then exactly sixteen days later, my name was being called to pack out.

"Mr. Deters, I've been up here working in R&D for the last few days. I am glad that you are finally getting out of here."

"Ms. Clarke," I said with excitement.

"Honey it's me and ain't too much about me gonna change. You gotta start eating Baby. You've lost quite a bit of weight. I know that losing your Mother was rough on you but you gotta bounce back now, you hear?"

"I swear, I'm trying. I really am Ms. Clarke."

At this time, I was returning the jail issued clothing, jumpsuit, socks, drawers and bed linens. I had already been given back my personal clothing. I figured

Ms. Clarke was goosing at how fly I was in some normal attire. I was rocking a pair of Red Bottom sneakers by Christian Louboutin and at $995-$3200 a pair, my Gucci jeans and t-shirt didn't even matter. Nor my Atlanta Falcons fitted.

We were in the back of the property room and Ms. Clarke looked at me then used a finger over her mouth as if to say, "Hush!" Puzzled as I was, I threw all of the clothes and linen into the desired baskets and watched her intensively.

She removed a piece of paper that had been folded down into a small square from her bra. I damn near drooled on myself as I watched with anticipation. Ms. Clarke grabbed a piece of tape from the counter while looking at me so seductively. She licked her lips and when she stepped closer to me, I felt the heat from her breath, on the tip of my nose. She reached into my pants with one hand and then followed with the other hand. I stiffened when she wrapped the small piece of paper around the shaft of my dick. Without a doubt, I became hard from the gentle touch of her soft hands. This was nowhere near what I expected.

"Don't let nobody see that, do you hear me Sweetie?"

"OK I murmured."

Ms. Clarke leaned in and kissed me on my lips so slow and softly. She pulled away from me, sucking on my bottom lip. Then she smiled and stepped towards the door, I was so shell shocked that I moved in silence and followed her so willingly.

"Don't give these people any trouble Honey. You hear me?"

"Yes mam, I do."

"I don't agree at all with how they wouldn't let you go to your mother's funeral services. That was the craziest situation I ever heard of in my life."

"It crushed me Ms. Clarke," I said as she held the door open for us both to exit.

About forty feet away on the other side of the waiting area, stood two Alexandria Virginia Sheriffs. One was tall and dark skin, the other was a chubby middle aged, white man with a bald head.

"Take this break you are getting Honey and get your life together for your Mother, get your life together Honey." She said in a very low tone.

"OK Ms. Clarke," I whispered. "You take care."

Those were the last words I spoke to her. Afterwards, I was handcuffed and shackled, then transported into an awaiting van. Staring out of the window, I examined damn near every single tree. I looked down and into every single car that we passed or that drove fast enough to pass us. The Potomac River looked good enough to swim in and I dreamed of just that as we rode over the Woodrow Wilson Bridge.

Chapter 9

The Virginia Commonwealth and the sign on the
I-495 highway entering the state read, *Virginia is for
Lovers.* Anything else and that surely meant it wasn't
a good place for a nigga at all. So many had gotten
over that bridge or the 14th Street Bridge but never
fortunate enough to make it back. A many of black
men, are still trapped in the Virginia system, wishing
that they never crossed either bridge.

The conviction rate in Virginia is just as high
as the Feds and if sentenced for a crime you are
forced to do 85% of any time given. The reason for
venturing into such a place has always been because
Washingtonians had been doing so for years. The money
doubled or even tripled in some areas.

Sure enough, people would pay twice as much
for drugs. Dimes went for thirty in a lot of places.
Working halves were broken down and two hundred
and fifty dollars was easily made off of them back
in the day. Off of one ounce of crack, you could see
thirty five hundred dollars or anywhere close to it. A
kilo went for whatever price you put on it above the

average. Wasn't anybody trying to travel to get it? The value for drugs was surely different and if you got caught, that was another story all together and a price to surely pay.

I took risk ever since I was introduced to the game. At the age of thirteen, I vowed to be in it to win it. No matter if it meant crossing a bridge or swimming through a river to grab a dollar. I hustled to survive and against all odds I was still out to win. In spite of any boundaries set by any one area, I was running and hoping to flee as I bounced throughout DC, Maryland, and Virginia. I wasn't doing it on my own accord but I knew that soon enough, my time to shine was coming.

The Alexandria Detention Center was packed. I was given a mattress and thrown in a cell on the floor. At any other time, I would've surely protested. Only I was exhausted from the travel and had been in the booking area for so long that it felt good as hell to just be able to get some rest.

The old guy on the concrete slab above me, rolled over, made eye contact and took his old ass back to sleep. I went to the toilet and took out the folded piece of paper and tried to read it under the glow of moonlight that was shining through the small window. I spotted the name Gertrude C. and a phone number that I couldn't clearly make out, on one side. With no intentions to ever call Ms. Clarke, I smiled and dropped the small piece of paper in the toilet. The only thing on my mind was getting my case heard. So, I lay down under the wool blanket and got some sleep.

After three weeks passed, and I was transported to the courthouse, it was more than a relief. I had a court appointed lawyer that seemed as if he was happy when I told him that I was facing fifteen years in the Feds. Somehow, the Judge was affected by it also.

"Mr. Deters, I am sorry to hear about the pending Federal charges. You are surely facing a substantial amount of time. I am going to terminate your probation here and Mr. Deters . . ."

"Yes mam? I mean, yes your Honor?"

". . . I wish you luck young man. Court adjourned. You may be remanded to the custody of the Sheriff."

At that point, I was still confused to what had actually happened in the courtroom. So, I sat back and enjoyed the ride as the van left the courthouse. With a little bit of speed, it swung through an area in Alexandria called Up-Town. We stopped at a stop sign on Queen Street and there were several people on the corner trying their best to see inside of the van. As if the windows hadn't had the slight tint or the metal fencing over them.

We pulled off and a few young chicks, pushing strollers waved. Some kids raced on bicycles alongside of us as if they could paddle with the speed of the vehicle.

After whizzing through another area called the South side, we cruised down North Payne Street. There was a cemetery on one side and several row houses on the other. The Sheriff hit the horn three times, while driving down the block. We drove to the end of the street and made a right. The driver took a non-service road through a sanitation plant.

Before long we were back at the sally port of the jail. As each individual stepped out of the van and onto a milk crate, you could see the relief in every face. The ride was not the most comfortable when in handcuffs and shackles. The seats seemed as if they were always too damn close.

As each man or woman stepped into the search area, they were questioning the Deputies about the outcome of their cases. One of the four officers held a clipboard with the adjudication of each person. The doors to the van were open and I was listening hard.

Apparently, the Deputy got fed up with the questions and just blurted out everybody's business.

"Ms. Bridgette Flemming, three years and child support.

Ms. Yolanda Green, RELEASE on personal recognizance.

Mr. Deon Quarles, time served, RELEASE.

Mr. Michael Marble postponed until the 19th.

Mr. Maurice Knight, ninety days, community service.

Mr. Asim Deters, probation terminated, RELEASE."

As I heard it, I wasn't even sure it was real. Everybody who had went to court had received light sentences and I was in the mix of all that. I never reported after I had been issued the probation and ironically, I was being terminated. With everything I had, I fought hard as hell to conceal my excitement. I went through the initial search again as we entered the booking area.

When I made it back up to my floor, 4G was quiet and the majority of the men were engulfed in the TV. They were watching videos on BET I could hear Wale. A like that young rapper who put the entire DMV on the map. He was going on one.

"Gotta get back to the D, we finally famous."

Instead of sitting down to sing along with the young soldiers, I went to the phone. I gave the number that I had for April a try and once again, I got the recording. Without a doubt, the phone was still disconnected.

I was so jittery that I couldn't sit down, so I paced the tier for about an hour. My mission was to stay sucka free. The section 8 Mob, the New Projects, 3000, Duke Street, the South Side and The OG Mob, kept a lot of tension in the air. I wasn't ducking no rec. Yet I was damn sure trying to stay out the way of those Virginia neighborhood rivals that were representing their areas· At least long enough to make it out of the door·

When the Deputy called out my name and badge and baggage, I didn't waste any time getting to the front desk with my property bin· I eventually made it back down stairs to the booking area and was issued my clothing· The same Red Bottom sneakers, Gucci jeans and t-shirt, I was sure enough glad that I had my Atlanta Falcons fitted because I was in need a haircut bad·

Me and another guy were being released and as he tied the strings to his white, Chuck Taylor Converse, All Stars, he looked up at me·

"I thought you were waiting to go back out to · · ·"

"Nah! Slow down Playa·" I said while cutting him off·

"Oh!" He responded· "My bad young soldier· I'm Joe and if you don't remember, I'm the older cat that they put you in the cell with when you first got in·"

"OK Yeah! Joe James, I remember you·"

This man was well into his fifties· Yet he had the spunk of a young dude; the colors of coffee with a little creamer, medium build, with a bald head and a long grey beard·

Older fellas had laid the Game down for us to be able to play the way we play today· Plenty of them same older dudes have been known to dress how they wanted· So, I didn't think twice about his straight leg, Jordache jeans and V-neck, white T-shirt·

"I see things are going your way·"

"I would say so, if I make it through that door·" I responded·

"You will· I've got my woman out front and I will get her to give you a ride if you need one· That is the least thing I could do for you," said Joe as he scratched at a stain on his jeans·

"I appreciate it·"

"I've been down since 1970. I'm a convict soldier and I'm down for whatever the hell will help another convict."

"Wow!" Excuse me for even asking. What did you do?"

"Well, they say that I cut the police head off, at Lorton. For years, the rumor was that I cut his head off and put it in the damn sewer."

"Yeah! That's serious."

"It would be if it was true. Let me just tell you that I did kill a nigga. That is definitely true. How many is a whole different story. I took care of a muthafucka on the street and in the pen. A man has always got to be willing to take care of his business."

"I can dig it."

"All in all, I managed to give these people the majority of my life. I've been in since the dining halls were segregated and separated. I remember when prison was prison, for real. When rats barely existed because they were being killed at an all-time rate. Now, the Federal system is heavily populated with them and you can't tell who the hell is who."

"Yeah! I'm hip Joe."

"However things go for you son. You gotta walk out of those doors and live every day of your life, like it's golden. That's right! You gotta enjoy every damn minute and live like it's your last day. Like a car on the freeway, you gotta keep it moving son and switch lanes while you're doing it."

Minutes later, we were both called over to a desk and asked several questions to verify our identity. Social security numbers, birthdates and our thumb prints were given as well. Afterwards, we were told to sit down again, while our names were ran through the National Crime Information website, on the computer. That process didn't take long and apparently didn't show any outstanding warrants, holds, or detainers in any other jurisdictions.

As me and Joe stood at the double exit doors, sweat ran down my sides. Butterflies swam all around my stomach. Then the Lieutenant looked directly at me.

"You alright?" The older brown skin woman asked. "You look like you're not sure you wanna go on the other side of those doors. I mean, most people are already smiling. Or at least looking like this is the way that their supposed to be going."

"Huh?" I questioned with shock.

"Oh! He's still trying to get that nasty ass taste out of his mouth from that meal we just ate. Those damn beans sure weren't the best. Open those doors up Ms. Smith and let us up out of here. I've been in chains a little too long Sweetie. My time is all the way up."

"I totally agree Mr. James," she said with a smile. "You two gentlemen don't come back now."

As we waited I perspired extremely hard, I was nervous yet a very few feet away from freedom. The both of us stared hard while Ms. Smith spoke into her walkie-talkie.

"CBJ 1, pop door number 1 and door number 2. I have two inmates being released 3421009; this is Lieutenant Smith, copy?"

"CBJ 1 copies."

She smiled and watched us exit through both doors. Neither one of us looked back.

Chapter 10

The air of the free world, hit me in my face with an extremely hard blow. It was pure pleasure and every bit of what I had hoped and longed for. The sun had started to go down and it was damn near dark outside. Although I had made it out of those doors, I hadn't made it through the last security post that surrounded the outside perimeters of the jail.

Joe and I walked quickly as possible towards the gate that was monitored by one last Deputy. Ironically, we slid through that same entrance and exit with ease. There were several vehicles lined along the street and we hurried past most of them in an attempt to find his lady friend.

Suddenly, a horn and a set of car lights blinked several times. Joe smiled and I signaled in the direction of a 2011, black, Ford Explorer. A beautiful long haired, caramel complexion, older woman, opened up the driver's door and began frantically waving. She was smiling from ear to ear and so overwhelmed with joy.

"Joe! Oh Baby, you made it! Joe Baby!"

"Clarissa!" He yelled.

As they engaged in a strong embrace, filled with tears, joy and definitely love, I slipped past both of them and into the back seat of the truck. They held each other for a minute or two and kissed one another so passionately. Joe pushed her back and examined all of her beauty then they jumped into the truck.

"Clarissa, I'm sorry Honey. I was so excited to see you, I almost forgot. This here in the back is my partner Jake."

"Hello Jake," she said as she looked in the rearview mirror at me while still smiling so very hard.

"I'm just a little excited that my man has finally made it back to me."

"I understand Sweetie. If it's not too much to ask, after you get good and away from this jail, is there any way I could use your phone?"

"Sure," said Clarissa. She leaned over to kiss Joe for the umpteenth time. Then she started the truck and sped up and out of the parking lot.

"Jake, I have the Ford My Touch system. Modern technology is so brilliant. Give me the number."

Quickly I responded, "It's (703) 555-2355."

A few seconds later, the phone began to ring through the truck speakers. Both me and Joe were in awe but neither one of us said a word.

"Jake just talk honey. They can hear you."

"Hello," said a female voice, loud and very clear.

"Niki, it's me and I am not too far from you. I done made it out and I need you to meet me at the King Street Metro Station."

"What? When boy?"

"Right now. I will be there in the next fifteen minutes."

Somehow, she knew not to ask any damn questions. After the phone call, I rode with my head leaned up against the head rest. I was vibing off the Estelle CD that Clarissa had playing. A singer I had never heard before from London whom sounded real soulful. As the bass beat, she sang some deep and heart wrenching music.

Joe passed me a Newport and the first pull of it had spent my head in every direction. I was dizzy for a second or two. Then I continued to inhale and exhale and tried to enjoy the smoke.

It didn't take long at all to get to the Metro Station. I wasn't at all comfortable with meeting her there. A tunnel sat not too far from the entrance, leading to the Federal Courthouse of the Eastern District. Therefore, a lot of the traffic going to and from where working class citizens of all types including lawyers, legal aides, secretaries and so forth and so on.

By the time we got there, Joe had exchanged shoes and clothing and had the appearance of an all new guy. He had on a pair of all black Nike boots, a Hugo Boss hoodie and a pair of Hugo Boss jeans. His outfit looked great but the smile he had on his face was even better.

"It feels too good to be out here young soldier."

"You ain't never lied Joe."

"You've gotten the break of a lifetime. Use it and whatever you do, keep switching lanes on them."

"I've got one question?" I asked while staring at the jazzy old fella, while we stood in the parking lot, outside of the truck.

"Go ahead, ask it."

"How in the hell did you figure?"

"I told you, I've been in since seventy boy. Not only that, but the night you came in that cell, you assumed that I was asleep. After you went to the toilet and got back in the rack, I got up to take my insulin. You obviously didn't flush the toilet, because your business was floating on the water."

"Damn! So, I guess · · ·"

"You ain't gotta guess shit," said Joe as he cut me off. "What I saw that night was a body attachment sheet, showing how you were supposed to be handed over to the custody of the US Marshalls for a Federal Hold. The obvious reason why you were able to slip out of the doors today, three days before your Federal court hearing. What I saw was that same business go down in a swirl. I told you son, I'm a convict and I've done enough time to stay the hell out of the business of others."

"I respect that and all in a nutshell, I gotta say that I definitely respect your G shit Joe James."

"We've been here rapping for far too long. You need to get a jump start on those people. By Monday morning, there will be a nationwide manhunt for your black ass. When you don't show up in that court room, the Feds are gonna kick in every door of every relative or acquaintance that you ever had contact with while in custody."

"Yeah! This is gonna be serious."

"It's your life, so take it serious."

Me and Joe gave each other five and a long hard embrace. After the brief bonding, he forced me to take a one hundred dollar bill from him. I could only assume that it had been amongst all the gifts that his lady friend Clarissa had waiting for his long and definitely, anticipated release.

To make myself seem unseen, I sat down at a bus stop in front of the station. Then after a few minutes went by, I noticed Niki pulling into the parking lot in her white, 2010, Audi A8. The car looked good, sounded good and although it demanded plenty of attention, sitting on all that chrome, she demanded more when she stepped out of it.

Niki's hair was whipped up and over into a unique style of some layered curls that complemented her dark chocolate, brown skin tone. With a duffle bag over her shoulder, the strap ran directly in between her breast, separating a not too large pair of twins. As Niki walked the bounced on her hip, showing off another one of her prize assets. Her boots were all the way like that. She was rocking a pair of peep toe design, ankle boots by

Gucci. Niki had on a black sweater with a ruffled collar and some black tight fitting pants.

Trying to seem as inconspicuous as possible, I let Niki sashay from the car to the entrance of the station. Then after I watched her look around aimlessly for a while, I slid up on her.

"Oh my God! Boy you done got big!"

"Hey girl! Give me a hug." I said with open arms.

Our embrace lasted maybe more than either of us intended. We stood there holding one another real tight. There was a lot of pain inside the both of us. Some longing and a whole lot of regret for things having went the way they did.

"Look what you did to my shirt. Tell me how the hell you pulled this one off."

"I'll explain it to your ass one day. Right now ain't the damn time. Your mascara is running." I said with a smile.

Niki wiped under her pretty brown eyes, "Guess we both got a little emotional with your crazy ass. Here take this." Niki said as she handed me an all-black duffle bag from off of her shoulder.

"What's good?" I asked.

"I threw a few things together that I figured you might need. Stop asking me stupid shit boy. Just take the bag and here is a smart trip card for the train. Get on it and get your ass up out of here."

"OK." I said while adjusting the bag on my own shoulder and taking the card from her hand.

"This damn sure isn't the place for you."

"I love you girl."

"Stop all that sucka shit. Just call me when you get in the city. Get outta here."

"I'll do that Babygirl. I'm gone."

When I made it to the top of the platform, I could look down and was able to see the parking lot area. Niki sped off and I watched her red brake lights, until she drove completely out of sight.

Chapter 11

Every odd face was an enemy. I had suddenly become so sour. I couldn't smile, I wouldn't smile and for the likes of me, I didn't want to smile. I much rather wanted to get clear away from the Virginia area. So, as the lights on the platform blinked, I stood and anticipated the coming train. With a sign reading, *Addison Road*, I slid on the blue line and quickly grabbed a seat in a corner.

After riding for a while, I slid the zipper back and peeped into the duffle bag. With it on my lap, I surveyed its contents without opening it all the way. There was an all-black outfit of some sort, a pair of Nike boots, a pair of black leather gloves and blue steel, ·40 caliber handgun. There was no question that Niki had packed the duffle. She had made sure that the weapon was loaded and an ounce of some exotic was rolled up and stuffed in the trigger space.

I took the gun out, after I was sure that nobody was looking in my direction. I put the exotic in my pocket and slid the Forty in my waist band. Just as I was about to zip the bag shut, I saw the money sticking out of one of the jeans pockets. I reached in the back pocket and there was ten, one hundred dollar bills and a pack of Backwoods. Nothing else could solidify my comfort ability at that moment.

I leaned back, the train zipped down into a tunnel. Before long, I was in the good ole District of Columbia. That's right! The nation's capital, home of the White House and every other government office or building that had a little power behind this fucked up ass country. The Library of Congress, the United States Capital Building, the United States Patent Office, the United States Treasury Department and a countless amount of other buildings that are controlled by politics.

Barrack Obama, the first black president was inaugurated here. The first statue to be built on the Mall, honoring a black man. In fact, the late great, Dr. Martin Luther King Jr. and all his effort to stop segregation is commemorated right here. I was born here and within this same city, I had known a many of good men who died. Died while they struggled to keep their heads above water. Died while hustling to feed their stomachs, their addictions, and more importantly some just trying to feed their damn families.

Get It How You Live! A real life motto. A many of DC streets were gritty. There were four sections, South East, South West, North East and North West. Every one of them held its own. Get caught loafing on the wrong side and you would just become another one of the Districts, countless homicides.

I wasn't sight-seeing nor did I have a lot of time for any bullshit. I needed to eat and sit still for a minute while I gathered together my thoughts. The sun had disappeared and it was getting later and later. After getting off the train at Metro Center, I caught a cab to another one of my sister's spots, right there in North West.

Tameka stayed in the Tyler House, right on North Capital Street. A tall high rise, project building, filled with some of the fattest and finest baby mommas of all walks of life. While walking in front of the building, you would see young kids posted in front on the wall. Some would speak.

"What up Slim?" Others would ask, "Wuz good Moe?"

Some mugged on you and others tried to hustle you what they sold. From cigarettes to weed, to coke and who knows what else.

Security was faking real good like. So, I had to put my head down and walked into the building real fast like I was on my way home from some place. I took to the left hallway, then passed a day care, swung right and another quick left and got on the elevator. There were a few young chicks on it and a snotty nose little boy who was mean mugging me. Made me feel like I owed his little ass some cookies or candy.

Everybody had gotten off. Instead of going up to the fifth floor, the elevator went into the basement. When the doors opened, there was about twenty dudes crouched down in the midst of a dice game. A few stood up and I didn't see one smiling face in the crowd of Jordans, New Balance, Phoam Posits and many North Face jackets. The doors closed back and I felt a little relief for a second. I was strapped but I was damn sure outnumbered and not in the mood for no gunplay.

In this building, you get off on the wrong floor and never know what the hell might happen. Each one was known for something different. Sweet Tina sold O cups on the 8th floor. The candy lady lived at 403 and Ms. Butterfingers had plenty of snacks, candies and then some. Little Laquisha sold the good, good green on the 6th floor and the pills, coke and dope were on the 7th floor.

The Taylor House was off the chain and at any time you would see little kids zipping through the hallways making runs for their mommas. Carrying flat irons and hair curlers was the normal. Dragging a younger brother or sister with them was most times mandatory. Even borrowing sugar or bread was asked of Momma. Just a bunch of moving about in the confinements of where they lived. Trying to get ahead, trying to get by.

My little sister Tameka wasn't home and I was dead ass tired. So, I slid into the stairwell and after sitting for so long, I fell asleep, with the duffle bag between my legs. I was tired and although I had my hand in my dip rested my gun; I had no business at all dozing off right there. Pipe heads, vagabonds and so forth frequented the stairwells. I would be lucky to wake up with my shoes still on my feet. Then there were those who blew in the stairwell because they preferred not to smoke in their apartments around their babies.

Chapter 12

I awoke at 3:20 a.m. to the giggling and chattering of three bad women.

"Damn boo! You ain't gotta do it like this. If she put you out, she crazy as shit." Said a light skin female with hazel colored eyes.

She was wearing a skin tight red dress that fit her fine ass real well. She had on some six inch heels by Louis Boutin that look like they had glass heels on each shoe. Whoever did her extensions could have done a better job. She was still, jive like that and she had an attitude like she knew it.

"Girl he so fine, he supposed to be on the couch."

"Yeah! You right DaDa and I'm gonna leave you and Paris Hilton, in this damn stairwell to play with his fine ass. Yes! Before I fuck around and be sleeping on a fucking couch my damn self. Yall know Doughnut is downstairs watching my babies. I gotta go get me a shower and let him beat it before he goes to work."

As I cleaned my eyes and took in a deep breath, I could smell the still fresh odor of a dipper. Whoever that pretty eyed chick was in that dress, left down those stairs with a hell of an impression. Her phat ass bounced as she took each step and I watched her weave bounce and her booty jiggle until she was out of sight.

"Yall sure as hell caught me loafing," I said in disbelief.

"What the hell you doing in the hallway anyway Boo?" Asked the female.

"My lil sister ain't home and I was dead ass."

"I'm DaDa and this quiet, white looking Bitch right here is called by so many names. Paris Hilton, White Chick, White Bitch and off the no bullshit, she all the way like that. Instead of you lying up in this pissy hallway, you can bring your fine ass with us."

DaDa was every bit of 5'4 and a caramel color. Her eyes were a natural brown but slanted in the way that gave her such a pretty eyed stare. She had a perfect set of titties for her little frame. At 131 pounds and a 36C, it was just all so healthy.

That night, I noticed her cleavage and was admiring the hitting ass, low neck line, Fendi sweater she had on. The cream colored khakis were as if they were painted on. It was a real nice sight. She had her hair wrapped in a cream and black Fendi scarf.

"DaDa you don't even know this nigga name."

"I'm Spider," I responded.

"Ooh! Does that mean that I should be real careful not to get caught all up in your web," said DaDa with a devilish grin.

"Girl you a mess. Since you trying to get life and giving out invitations, yall come on," said Paris Hilton. "Finish up them damn cigarettes and come the hell on cuz I'm locking the damn door."

When we all entered the apartment, my eyes got big as hell. The pad was laid out. Real nice English leather furniture. A glass coffee table and a fifty inch flat screen on the far wall. Spider lamps draped over the tall green elephant plants. Ferns hung down from the ceiling in certain areas and several mirrors decorated the walls.

Ms. Paris Hilton floated through the living room and her tall ass, disappeared in the darkness of the hallway. She hollered out.

"Bitch, you know where the hell the blankets are. Yall don't let nobody else up in my shit."

All we heard was a door slam in the distance and lock. DaDa bent down and took off her heels. I could see the French pedicure on her toes, glistening from the light off the flat screen television. As she stepped through the living room, over what appeared to be three different women, I followed her. The living room was looking like a great big ole slumber party.

On one couch were a heap of blankets and a set of cheeks with red boy shorts that hung out and off the edge. The pillows from the love seat were underneath two of the other females who lay sprawled out on the floor. It was an all-out room full of pussy. With my eyes full of legs, panties and whatever pieces that they let hang out of their blankets I was enjoying the sights. What man wouldn't?

Two bright red bunk beds made it more than clear that we had entered a room belonging to not one but two little kids. Their toys were all scattered about. ABC blankets covered both beds. DaDa shut the door behind us and locked it. Then she led me across the hardwood floor. After I sat on the bottom bunk, DaDa clicked on a television with a built in DVD player that sat on the only dresser in the room. Nothing specific played but I remember using the light to examine her tiny waist and the beautiful curves on her body. She turned around, walked towards me and stopped directly in front of me them said softly.

"Spider, I'm gonna get comfortable Boo and I hope you can control yourself being around a woman with barely any clothes on."

"Damn! You say that like I'm gonna nut up or something. Don't come for me. You a bad chick and you dripping a lil swag juice but I ain't geeking Ma. I'm a certified nigga and I got that swag goo for real."

"Well do something for me with your swagged out ass," DaDa said, while allowing me to see her smile, revealing a perfect set of teeth in the dim light.

"What's that sexy?" I asked.

"Unzip the back of this sweater for me, so I can breathe. After a while this shit make a bitch feel like its cutting off some circulation or something.

DaDa turned around and I did what she asked. I could smell a faint sweet aroma of an alluring fragrance. Not only did she take off her sweater but she stepped out of her pants as well. Her body dimensions were unbelievable. The black laced, boy shorts bit into her caramel colored ass cheeks and looked so tantalizing.

I spun her back around to face me and noticed how bad she was. I wasn't disappointed that's for sure. A perky set of nipples were staring back at me. A thin line of hair trailed from her stomach on down just below her navel. DaDa had no stretch marks, no blemishes and nothing sagged. I had stumbled across the right damn thing that night. Or so I thought any way.

When I reached out to touch DaDa, she slapped my hand away and said abruptly, "Why don't you take off your shoes Honey and get real comfortable. You ain't gotta rush, I ain't going nowhere. Take off your shirt and relax."

I took the pistol out and slipped it in the duffle bag. As I did so, she just watched. After I took off my pants and shirt, she folded them neatly and set them along with her belongings next to my bag. To assure me that I was safe, she scooted it all right over to the side of the bed, just in case I needed to grab it or something.

Together we got on the bottom bunk bed and lay on a blanket that felt like it had candy stuck to it in a few areas. We used it to cover ourselves with. For a while, I just held onto DaDa's small frame tightly and used my body to warm hers. We played footsies for a while and snuggled. It had been a long time since I had held a woman so I relish in the moment, just enjoying the comfort of closeness.

Then I leaned in trying to kiss DaDa and when I did so, she moved every which way out of my reach. I tried it again and she just wouldn't let our lips meet. I wasn't sure if my breath had been stank or what, so I leaned over to the side of the bed, blew out a quick breath and sniffed. No stank smell and didn't know what the hell was up.

While I lay there thinking about something as frivolous as a kiss, DaDa began to reposition herself in the bed. She went under the cover and after taking my dick out of the hole in my boxers, she made me gasp. I felt the condom roll off her tongue and she worked it down and around my shaft with her mouth. She created an astonishing big smile on my face. A few minutes before she was talking shit. Now I was laid back getting brain and enjoying every single bit of it.

DaDa didn't skip a beat. She was slurping and sucking so loud that I used the remote control to try and drown out her effortless work. At some point, she pulled the cover off her head. Afterwards, I was able to look down at her and watch. She noticed and she looked back up at me with a devilish stare. Teasingly, DaDa beat my dick all over her face. Playfully she smacked it up against her cheeks, forehead and up against her lil pudgy nose. Then she deep throated it and held the dick in her throat.

I watched in awe as DaDa spit on my dick to give it plenty of lubrication. She was slow, then fast. DaDa got aggressive, yet she was attentive. Damn! She was good, so good that I couldn't do anything but enjoy the pleasure. I was so hard that it made it easy to slide down on, when she mounted me. I could feel her warm insides and all of DaDa's juices flowing. Then she began to gyrate her hips and rode me like she was riding a rodeo style bull. I thumped my own hips back and DaDa worked even harder to meet my rhythm.

"Let me fuck you from the back," I whispered.

"No! Just relax Daddy, I got you."

So, that's exactly what I did. She took full control. DaDa grabbed onto the poles of the upper bunk and held onto them, while she worked. I let out a sigh and tried to keep up with her speed. That wasn't enough, she turned around and gave it to me in the cowgirl position and fucked me some kind of good.

"Tell me when you're about to cum," said DaDa.

"OK Baby. Just throw that pussy."

"Yes Daddy! Tell me you like it."

"I love it."

"Good." She said then moaned and grunted a few times.

"Here it cum."

"When?"

"Now," I murmured.

DaDa hopped off the dick, ripped off the condom and jerked the dick frantically. When I released, she caught it all over her face. It was something straight out a porn DVD. It was quick, good and supposed to last a whole lot longer.

After we both rested for a while, she cleaned us both up with a soapy rag. Then together, we sipped out of a small pint size bottle of Grey Goose. DaDa lay with her head on my chest. Just as I began to doze off, she nudged me in my side.

"I usually charge a muthafucka $3000 an hour for what you just got."

"Say what?"

"You heard me. As good as my pussy is; you think I'm giving it away for free?"

I looked down at her, "So, you snatched me out of the stairwell cuz you thought I was a trick?"

"No baby· Tricks pay to play·"

"Oh yeah!"

"Yeah! You ain't gotta pay because I like you and I'm hoping we can play together·"

"What the fuck are you talking about?"

"Nigga, I'm talking about the GAME· I like your fine ass enough to give you the ins and outs of some real to life shit·"

"What shit?"

"Some space age pimping shit Spider·"

I lightly pushed her off of me and sat up, resting my back on the wall· I looked down at this young bad, beautiful girl· She was so sexy, so young and so damn nasty·

"It's more than obvious, that your life isn't all together· I mean, sleeping in a fucking stairwell· Mine damn sure isn't· Instead of helping this white chick pay all her fucking bills and take care of her kids, I want a life of my own·"

"So, you figure, you could get that with me? We just met DaDa and who the fuck do you think I am?"

"I don't know but I'm ready to take a fucking chance," she said while starting to cry·

I stared at her while tears began to stroll down her face· She was so beautiful yet something ugly had stained her soul· DaDa had a pain embedded within the depths of who she was and why her life had turned out the way it had been·

It was at that time, with a face full of tears, that she let me lean in and kiss her· Slow delicate pecks on her cheeks· I kissed her eye lids but she kept crying· I could taste her salty tears on my lips· Then finally she let our mouths meet· Slowly we kissed and savored the taste of one another·

That kiss was magical yet it felt like it wasn't supposed to happen· It was dirty· Even she felt something a little bit wrong about it· Abruptly, she snatched away from me, right in the middle of our tongue locking embrace. DaDa leaned over the bed and then searched through her pants until she had found what she was looking for.

"Here, this is yours Daddy."

I reached out and accepted two folded stacks of money that had been bound by rubber bands. I didn't say anything because I didn't know what the hell to say.

"Spider, do you know anything about computers?" DaDa asked while sniffling.

"We used to use them when I was in the Feds for that short lil stint of time, I did."

"For what?"

"I got caught loafing with some drink, shooting down the BWI Parkway. I can type a lil bit why wuz up?"

"Baby, I'm gonna show you how we gonna get rich off the internet and do some space age pimping. Everything is on the computer now and we gonna be on it, selling some of this good pussy."

With her back hand, DaDa wiped the snot from her pudgy little nose. As if I hadn't seen it.

"You nasty girl and you are crazy," I said with a smile.

She smiled and responded, "I'm serious."

I scooted back down in the bed and DaDa snuggled up under me closely.

She backed that thang up on me until the wee hours of the following morning.

Here I was running for my life and I had just coincidentally run into DaDa and a shit load of other mess. I wasn't signing up to be no damn pimp and thought I was just lucky enough to be getting a good piece of pussy.

Chapter 13

I never made it to my sister's house. Together, we left with absolutely no place to go. I had explained to DaDa everything that had happened to me up until then. She acted as if it wasn't nothing and she was out to prove that she was down for whatever.

I was lost and trying so desperately to piece together the puzzles of my own misconstrued ass life. Now being led in a whole new damn direction, switching lanes with a bad young female who knew what the lick was really hitting for.

We posted up in a cheap motel on New York Avenue called Budget Inn. DaDa turned a few tricks while I lay up, smoked plenty of green and plotted on a few low budget ass pimps who called themselves setting up shop.

I had wanted to get this one cat who had his shit show enough straight. A mint green Cadillac, sitting on gold vogues. His perm was laid down slick. He had four bad bitches working that spot and he was always talking shit and swallowing a bunch of spit.

Only Stay Down, had a whole lot more game than I expected and I figured I was better off leaving that fly muthafucka alone. I wasn't even all the way in the damn GAME and about to ruin my career before it even got started.

One night while DaDa was out and about, I stood outside of my room smoking a cigarette and Stay Down had pulled my coat tail.

"Young nigga, I see you've started a team. I like the move and I'm acknowledging that you can definitely go to the actual championship but you gotta play Baby play. Every team has a great manager and your trying to receive every playa's best. So, you gotta be able to manage even if the score is 15-17, 20-0 or even 0-0. Young nigga you ain't the one running up and down the court, so while managing you gotta compensate your playas. New Jerseys, new shoes and trips that show you appreciate the winnings.

The GAME gets rough sometimes and you ain't gonna always win. Yet, it's a victory if you still got all your playas and they're with you til the end.

"Be safe out here and after the club is over, you'll see a few bona fide marks. Get your weight up and play Baby play."

I pondered on everything that he had to say to me that night. GAME has always meant to be sold not told and he gave that piece to me for free. Without a doubt I knew that from that point on I had to play my very hardest.

Me and DaDa grabbed a two bedroom apartment in North East. Right on top of the hill in between Foots and Eads Street. It was home for a while and the roaches were a large part the family. They ran about and every now and again, you could catch a few darting across a wall, either that or making their way about, in and around the kitchen cabinets.

Whenever I would lie on the couch some nights, I could hear a mouse or two rummaging through the trash can· I assume they had squeezed themselves under the back door that led from the kitchen down into the backyard· You could clearly see out of the window over the stove and into the alley that ran over to 60th Street·

Several young kids who stole SUVs would park them in our alley· There were Crown Vics·, Caprice, Impalas, a few trucks and several other cars with or without rims parked back there· Me and DaDa would sit and smoke Dank on the porch some nights, while those same wild ass kids put on one hell of a show· They would speed through that alley and up and down 58th, 59th or 60th and sometimes stop right at the top of the hill, overlooking Woodson Senior High School· Even with the blue bird in the sky and a bright light beamed down on them, they would be revving up the gas· Smoke could be seen as it went up into the air and a strong odor of burning rubber filled plenty of noses·

As a marked patrol car or two whipped up behind them, we would be choking, laughing and smoking while they sped off and teased with an incredibly high speed chase· After they took off you could hear tires screeching from afar· A lot of those crazy ass events started off from a carjacking or a simple truth or dare· Wild young teenagers taking some hell of a risk with their own lives and the vehicles and lives of others·

The lady across the street had a son named Phil and him and his little partner Oop got forty years behind such a spectacle· The ghetto streets of DC were unexplainable and the same streets, I grew to love· Often events happen that were spontaneous and events to be surely remembered·

We were in the hood and in spite of the kids selling dimes all up and down our street, or the hot cars that were parked in our alley, we were good· It's been said that you can't turn a whore into a housewife and maybe that was true· I was absolutely comfortable with the hitting ass job DaDa was doing with the spot we shared.

She cleaned and vacuumed regularly. The kitchen was only dirty whenever I left it like so. She ran my bath water and ironed my clothes, laying out my outfits daily. DaDa kept me so right that she pressed my drawers and sprayed my socks down with any one of my colognes.

I didn't have a housewife but I had everything I needed in her. She rolled my weed up and even sparked the lighter when I got ready to smoke. She did things to meet my every move. Then one night, DaDa explained to me exactly why she was my Bottom Bitch.

"Spider your feet are cold Daddy."

"Bitch if I'm cold then your fine black ass needs to do a better job of keeping me warm."

She smiled up at me, as she began to trace over the tattoos on my chest.

"It's about time that I give it to you straight."

"Say what it is then."

"Well, the money we've been getting is some jive small time figures Daddy and it's about time that we step the game up."

"Bitch what?" I asked with a twisted face.

"I mean. If you want to, we can do things a little different."

"What man don't want some more money? You need to explain your damn self DaDa."

She got up and with a pair of peach thongs that slid up in her ass even more, once she stood. DaDa looked back over her shoulder at me and then signaled with her index finger.

"Come on, I wanna show you something."

I glanced at her exposed breast and after staring at those perky little nipples of hers, I followed her.

"I know that you're at least computer literate. What I'm about to show you is so serious Daddy."

There was a computer, printer and fax machine installed and up in the dining room area. It was an inexpensive Dell PC and a 32 inch flat screen monitor. I had let DaDa convince me to spend about three grand on the little office set up. I had only used it every so often. I grew to like it because I could keep in touch with my brother Anthony and a few other homeys who were stuck on lockdown.

The Feds used a website called Corrlinks and through them, I received whatever emails I did. Then whenever I wasn't caught up, I would send certain messages back on the inside. Always trying to motivate or give my men a few words of encouragement. Just letting them know what was happening in the world.

I bounced down into the rolling leather chair in just a pair of green silk boxers. DaDa sat her little ass right on my lap and without any hesitation she began to hit the key pad. Her fingernails were peach with black designs to match her toes. I watched as her fingers moved quickly. She typed with so much speed that I didn't clearly recognize what she keyed in as I peeped over her shoulder.

"What is this?" I questioned as I stared up at the screen.

"It's one of many social networking sites."

"Oh yeah!"

"Yes," said DaDa. "This particular one is free and it's called, getithowulive.com pay attention to how it shows a various amount of list to choose from. Several things that people desire. Like jewelry, furniture, clothing, shoes, cars, preferences of men and women and even dates to choose."

I watched DaDa use the mouse to scroll up and down the screen. She clicked on several of displays and icons. I was amazed and sat and watched her in awe.

"Wow! That's serious," I said with enthusiasm.

"You damn right it is."

"Can you pick what city and state or area that you prefer them to be in?"

"Daddy check this out."

DaDa hit a few keys and a few pictures of some barely dressed females popped up on the screen. I scooted the chair closer so that we could both see more clearly.

"Yes," she said. "You can pick from what you see and scroll through these sites Daddy and select what you really want cities, states, men, women, transsexuals, fetishes, ages, race and more."

"Tell me how the hell could you and I capitalize off of something like this Lil Momma?"

DaDa turned on my lap and looked me directly in my eyes. Then in her soft tone she said, "We can tap into this computer world with some sure enough space age pimping and win like never before."

"Well, go ahead Bitch. Spit it out."

Getting up off of my lap, she continued, "You and I live in the Nation's Capital. We are surrounded by several politicians, as well as Congressman and government officials."

"Yeah!" I said. "Police, Federal officers, servicemen and a rack of other shit go on."

"Well Daddy those are the elite gentlemen who come into our city on a many of business trips and ventures. The same men who would love to be a lil risky, while away from their families and wives."

"I like that."

"No! They would like it more if they could get a piece of pussy or get their dicks sucked while they're here."

I smiled. "Your right. How the hell are we supposed to tie them into us and a computer and man you still got me fucked up Lil Momma?"

"The pictures you saw of those few females. Well, they become pictures of your bitches Daddy. You gather them up. Give them names and descriptions;

even post them with wild ass fetishes if you like· Candy enjoys eating a tootsie pop and always gets down to the center· She knows how many licks it takes for ya· Hit her up and ask her·"

"Bitch, we going straight to jail·"

"No! Because we camouflage what the hell we're doing by displaying how these lovely ladies would love to receive 300 roses for an hour of their time· Nothing more would make a working lady feel more appreciated than a flower, so forth and so on·"

"$300 an hour multiplied by ten bitches and eight working hours, plus fetishes, fantasies and other perverted acts·"

I closed my eyes for a second or two with my finger on my temple· In my head I did the math to that and some more· Trying my best to total what it would be if I gave it a good run for a couple of months strong·

"Wooh! I screamed· "Now that sounds like I might fuck around and be all right·"

DaDa smiled and licked her pink lips, as her cute little ass rested up against the desk· "After that Daddy, you can develop your own web page, design it and the sky is the limit· I told you, this is some space age pimping that will fuck around and put us on the moon·"

"Come here girl·"

I grabbed DaDa and squeezed her little ass some kind of tight· She squeezed me back and straddled my lap· Then she whispered in my ear, "America is full of freaks just waiting to blow money· Porn sites are the most visited sites in the world· Just imagine Daddy how many tricks are gonna visit us if they know they can fuck something like this·"

DaDa started gyrating her hips in a circular motion slowly· She leaned back and grabbed one of her breast· Then seductively, she leaned her head down and began to suck on her own damn nipple· What she did was start a fire that I wasn't gonna put out. Instead, we fell off into the living room and began fucking ravagely. Not one roach or mouse could get in between us. We engulfed ourselves in passion.

As I looked down at DaDa in the middle of our sexcapade, drops of sweat dripped down on her. She had been so reluctant to kiss me before but now it was as if she couldn't stop. With our tongues entwined, we sweat, we fucked and we worked hard to please each other all over that apartment.

There wasn't one thing we didn't do sexually. I even remember her telling me to twist her ass up like a pretzel. So, somewhere in the event of it all, I did just that. DaDa was so young, energetic, and limber and so damn good. She was my partner, my girl, my confidant and my Bottom Bitch.

Chapter 14

Once again, I had begun to switch lanes. My life had taken an all new damn direction. Me and DaDa were going full speed ahead and everything she had spoken of, was happening. Only there was plenty more to space age pimping then she explained.

DaDa had gotten us both some Dell laptops. They came with so many features that I was lost while trying to figure out how to operate my computer at first. DaDa had shopped around and supposedly gotten us a fair deal. With the laptops we were able to move and groove. If need be, we could monitor any of our computer business on our laps, while we were in a car, train, in a park or damn near anywhere.

Finding a bobble head or a roller was never a hard job. Yet we had to lure in some young wild females and be able to market what the hell we were doing, all at the same time. I had come up with something that I was sure would work. So, after I had spent some time making sketches and designing, I threw the idea at DaDa to see if she dug it or not.

"Look at this Lil Momma. I want you to check out my work." I said after walking into the bedroom and seeing her laying across the bed heavily into something on her computer.

The room was clean and it smelled wonderful. DaDa was famous for burning scented candles. I could smell the strong aroma of vanilla in the air. I stepped over towards the bed, noticing that she was wearing one of my sky blue button ups and a pair of those great, great, granny panties. To top it off, they were an awful goldish brown color. DaDa had her feet up rubbing them together over her ass. Somehow, she was still cute even in the most natural state.

"Daddy wuz up?" she asked, without looking up at me.

"I just threw it on the bed. Stop typing for a second girl."

DaDa hit a few more keys then glanced over, "Daddy what about this business card is supposed to get my attention? I do all the cleaning and this place ain't nowhere big enough for us to get a maid."

"Bitch! These cards are how we're gonna get money."

"How you figure Daddy? What the hell these cards and cleaning got to do with pimping?"

She rolled over and leaned off the bed, taking a sip from a Rock Creek grape soda that had been sitting on the night stand. After that she grabbed a bag of barbeque sunflower seeds. Then she sat in the middle of the bed next to her laptop, Indian style.

After I watched DaDa get comfortable, I spoke. "Look! I want you to post an ad on that HITMEUP. com that says, Mesmerizing Maids. You see how I've drawn this little picture of the maid vacuuming with her shirt hiked up?"

"Yeah."

"Well, we will higher fast ass little bitches to clean large houses. You'll actually post real ads to clean and charge four hundred dollars per home· You'll target wealthy, white collar families in and around the Metropolitan area·"

"Then what?" she asked curiously·

"Then you and these young bitches will clean and work hard as hell·"

"I ain't no fucking maid·"

"That's exactly what the hell I'm talking about, because none of those young bitches that you hire really wanna be cleaning no fucking houses for no damn chump change either, you dig?"

"What?"

"Yeah! Bitch you'll explain to those young spring chickens how they can make $150 a day working for you· That's the equivalent to about $18 an hour and an amount of money that not too many will complain about especially during the times of this crazy ass economy· Then after you and them start cleaning for a few high saditty folks, you convince the girls to drop these cards in the suit pockets of the men who's houses they clean·"

DaDa hadn't eaten one single sunflower seed· She sat the bag down and reached out to get the card that I handed her·

"This is a totally different card Daddy· Where in the hell did you get this Ladies Club shit from?"

"DaDa that is what you'll manage Baby· All of the ladies, every single bitch that has the potential to get out there and get some bread· So, to entice the men you'll even go as far as kissing some of the cards with your sexy lips and writing provocative little messages on them to encourage them to call·"

I had grown tired of standing for so long, so I sat down on the side of the bed·

"You crazy," said DaDa·

"I'm serious and it'll work· Most of those dudes are gonna call the numbers back· Especially if there are lip prints on them or names written in red or hot pink and so forth."

DaDa twisted her face at me saying, "I bet your nasty ass would call a Bitch back if you found a card in your pocket that said, *Lucky Lucy, call me so I can do what it do.*"

"You damn right · · · ·

Before I could get it out DaDa playfully smacked at my head. I weaved here theatrical punches and love taps. Then I grabbed her ass up and gave her a little affection. That was surely all she wanted.

Chapter 15

A few weeks went by and things were working real well for everybody. DaDa's iPhone was ringing off the hook and the clientele was all in the habit of spending good money. Instead of just me and DaDa, there were now six of us living in that small ass apartment. Some nights, I would hear a bitch scream because I had stepped on a body part trying to get through the living room or hallway.

There was September, a nineteen year old, fine ass brown skin, Ethiopian, with more hips than a little bit. She had been raped by her older cousin and her brother. When she told her crack head mother about the traumatic experience, her mother used her as a pawn and allowed older men to fondle her and molest her for money. At the early age of eleven, September had been having sex and had her first child at twelve years old. She wasn't sure who her son's father was. Yet she was destined to get money for him and her two daughters. Ironically, they all suffered from Crohn's Disease.

Candy was a pretty eyed, caramel skin complexion, exotic dancer at one time. She had danced for a club called Sensationable, in Laurel, Maryland. Candy hadn't been making but $70-$80 a night getting naked. After she paid out her cab fare, weed money and the club for letting her perform each night, her take in was damn near nothing. DaDa met her through one of the other girls and convinced her that she would see the light. Without that wig and with some new clothes, she came around eventually and her take in grew and grew.

Labymba was the prettiest, bow legged, dark skin chick that I had ever seen. She had brown eyes and a distinctive array of tiny beauty marks underneath both of them. Labymba was from Nigeria and could move her small framed body like a snake. Weighing in at 123 pounds and at the height of 5'4, she had to look up at me whenever she spoke. Her feet were small and yet so cute. She loved to be barefoot and would keep her toes painted in so many different colors and styles. Labymba teased about how much she loved for a man to suck on her toes. Always speaking about how it made her giggle. She was 23 with a son whom she vowed to get back from her mother once her money was right.

Fire was the freakiest of all freaks, straight out of South East. This girl was light skin and phat to death. Had an ass that poked out like some wide tires on a whip. Her face was filled with freckles and a few pimples. There was even a cute little gap in between her two front teeth. Fire was into whatever and however sexually. A few drinks, a little weed or some pills and it was no holds barred. Fire claimed that she could fuck any man and make him come back for more. Her clientele was proving that to be right but I halfway thought it was because she was a squirter. I figured that men probably loved to see her make a mess with her juices while she stared back at them with her green colored eyes.

Most nights, all of the girls would go out and do what it do. They would head out around 6:00 p.m. or so and I wouldn't see them until the wee hours of the morning. I could hear them all giggling, talking and chattering about most nights. A lot of their jibber jabbering was about their tricks and dates and some of the wild and crazy things that some of them were asked to do.

DaDa would come in my room and almost always fuck up the best part of a good ass movie. Interrupting me from seeing who the killer was or how the ending usually took place. With a fifth of some Remy VSOP or Remy 1738 in my hand and smoking on some of the best exotic, DaDa would pour money into my lap.

"Here Daddy, we had a great night."

"Bitch!" I would scream. "Go clean the fuck up! I don't want to talk to you or them with the smell of sex all up on you. Get out of my face and don't speak to me until you clean the fuck up. Brush your teeth and take a shower Bitch!"

On this particular night, I poured myself another drink, damn near wasting it. For some odd reasons, I decided to sip out of a glass.

"Yall stupid whores better be paying attention out there. On the channel 5 news tonight, they say another girl got murdered."

"Oh yeah!" DaDa screamed back over the sounds of running water.

"Yeah!" I said back in a loud tone to assure that I was being heard clearly. "They found this one over there on New York Avenue at that cheap ass Motel right over the bridge, the one over top of the Fish Market. She had been sexually tortured. Some freak ass fool, tied her up with all different color panty hoses. Then the fool sodomized her, raped her and shot her three times in the back of the head."

"Damn!" screamed DaDa.

"It was supposedly that stalker that they have been trying to catch for some time now. The same one they believe killed the girl who was walking her dog in Rock Creek Park.

I kept talking and eventually nodded off to sleep while the girls took showers, played in the tub and took turns getting themselves ready for bed. That particular night, DaDa and Fire both came and jumped in the bed with me. I sat up and listened to them for a little while and let them sip on the Remy. Then while the girls clipped my toenails, pushed my cuticles back and used a warm moisturizing lotion to massage my feet, I felt so relaxed from the lavish treatment that I started snoring and went out on the ladies.

Chapter 17

The girls were all working so very hard and money was starting to roll in· On a totally different night, Candy had gone hysterical about a trick· One of her dates had a fetish that she couldn't seem to comply with· When I got the phone call, I broke up out of the apartment and headed straight to the hotel· They were staying in the Marriot in Greenbelt, Maryland that could be seen from the highway· As I took the exit ramp, my adrenaline was supercharging me to think that a fool had gone psychotic and started beating on one of my ladies·

DaDa, Candy and Fire met me in the lobby· I was dunned in an all-black outfit and boots· I had been strapped and was ready to kill something·

"What the hell is going on?" I asked when I had gotten within hearing distance and several feet away from the front desk·

The girls didn't say a word· Instead, they all walked me back outside· Apparently, it was too much for the lobby area·

"Daddy it's Candy," said DaDa·

"What's going on?" I asked, looking around at all three of them.

They were all in some of their working outfits. Short skirts, low cut blouses, tight pants and heels. A lot of skin meant the chance a trick would pay a lot of money to see the rest.

With disgust written all over her face, Candy stated, "There is some shit I just ain't doing. Kill my muthafucking mother. I just ain't doing some shit."

"What the fuck? I was thinking that somebody was hitting on one of yall or some crazy ass shit like that."

"Nah Daddy," said Fire.

"Well, what the fuck is it that yall got me running down here for?"

"Like I said, there is some shit that I just ain't doing."

"How the hell did you get those scratches and that red mark on your face Candy?" I asked with frustration.

"Me and DaDa got into it. That bitch · · ·

"Fuck you!" DaDa screamed.

Immediately, I used my hands to separate both of them. "Hold the fuck up! Cuz I'll duct tape both of yall stank asses. Don't get outta pocket with me. Candy for the last time bitch, what the hell is this all about?"

"I had a trick who was trying to get me to do some downright nasty, crazy ass stuff."

"This old Gwala, Gwala, whipped out some plastic and laid on the floor in the Hotel room. Then he got naked and lubed up his whole body with some KY Jelly."

"And?"

"And then he wanted me to dance for him first as some crazy ass Calypso music played. After the first song, I had to stand over top of him naked as the second song played. Then squat down and duck walk from his head going all the way down to his feet and come all the way back up to his nasty ass face doing it."

"Doing what?" I questioned with a puzzled ass look.

"Duck walking and pissing on his old nasty ass."

I screamed, "Bitch! For $300 an hour, you should've shitted on his ass too! Farted and pissed and shitted again."

I smacked Candy upside her head and as she spent I kicked her directly in her ass. When I looked up DaDa and Fire were laughing too damn hard. Apparently it was a little more funny than anything else.

Pimping ain't easy and there were dudes who wanted to get fucked, tortured, pissed on and even tied up and beat. The worst thing that I ever heard of was a grown ass man with a pamper on wanting to suck a titty and masturbate at the same damn time. How could anyone get off on that?

Yet, who am I to say what turned somebody else on? Everyone had their own dislikes and likes. My job was to manage these young ladies while they worked. So, in spite of the wild and freaked out stuff that they endured, I had to encourage them to keep getting that money. Keep getting it while being safe and careful all at the same damn time.

Labymba started racking in a rack of paper. A lot of the clients had desired to see her more than anybody. She wasn't just fucking the shit out of them. She was absolutely beautiful. Labymba had been on a few trips with a few different high rollers to Las Vegas, New York, Mexico, Bahamas and France. Whenever the flights were jumping you could expect her to be asked for. Sometimes men would be seriously upset that they weren't able to see her at certain times.

I made sure that her hair and nails were done regularly. She would get Senegalese or African twist at the hair gallery in the upper part of North West on Kennedy Street. I don't remember any style costing under $180 but when she walked out of the spot, you could always see why her hairdo was worth so much. She looked so spectacular. Labymba had a shape that did wonders in a dress. No matter how good she looked, she could always talk to me.

"Spider, you have helped me in a lot of ways and I am grateful to have found a man like you."

"Labymba. I am not that good of a man sweetie. Once you get your life together, you're gonna need to find a strong, smart man to marry. A man who can provide for you and your son, more importantly, instead of a man like me, you must find a man with stability."

"You are speaking so right to me."

"I am and I don't want you to look for someone who does any of the things that I do."

Labymba looked up and into my eyes. "You are not a man who enjoys pussy. Why have you never taken any of my advancements? Why have you never tried to fuck me? You have not even asked me to suck on · · ·"

"Shut up! I won't ever but that is not because I don't find you attractive. You are absolutely beautiful."

"You don't mean that." Labymba said with discern.

"I do and I want you to know that just because a man doesn't have sex with you that should never determine yourself worth. You are like a rare African diamond in the foothills of South Africa and I am gonna show you how much you mean to me soon, I promise."

"You promise?"

"Yes! Now go to bed."

That particular conversation happens and was only one of the many we had late nights or early in the mornings. Sometimes Labymba, Candy, September, DaDa or Fire would need or just want to talk to me about certain things they may have had on their minds.

I spent time with the girls and each one was indeed different. For the most part, I was putting away paper. After I had spent whatever was necessary to buy all the girls clothes and shoes, then I would pay for them to get check-ups at a local doctor. I bought them all personal items like, douches, tampons, lotions, soaps, etc. I made sure that their hair and nails were always fresh. Through me and some of my many lectures, I gave the girls lessons on etiquette, manners, how to trick, trap and trim and how to be The Ladies Club.

Chapter 18

Me and the girls continued to get money. While doing so, I had hoped to get myself a passport and a fake ID so that I could get the hell up out the Country. With all the money, I was stacking it wasn't anything impossible. The question was whether I was gonna take DaDa with me or any of the girls for that matter.

My bank statement read $76,231 and I had handled most of my banking on line. With the use of my laptop, I was able to do so very much. Twice weekly, I made deposits to the Bank of America on Martin Luther King Highway. Then all throughout the week, I would make the necessary wire transfers I needed to have done. I had a few private accounts that I handled. Sometimes I would order different clothing for the girls or myself and had the items delivered whenever anyone of us wanted to step out in style.

A lot had changed and for a man in my predicament, it seemed as if it only got better and better. We all still shared the small apartment together. For many of us, we enjoyed the fussing, cussing and drunk pillow fights that caused us all to fall out in different places to sleep

Although I could finally afford the Panamera or any other type of luxury vehicle that I wanted, I knew that purchasing anything to ride around and floss in would be beyond stupid. Enough to actually ruin everything that I had worked so hard for. None of the girls were allowed to drive. DaDa had hired a girl just for that purpose. Yet I had never met her or got in the car with her. I personally kept from behind the wheel of a car because I was aware that being pulled over at any time would allow my capture to be relevantly easy for law enforcements. I damn sure wasn't interested in that.

I had been enjoying life so much that I wasn't thinking about getting caught. For the likes of me, I didn't see that anywhere in my future. All I saw were my feet sinking on the white sandy beaches of a place far away from the United States. A cold drink with an umbrella in it, with everything behind me, that ever seemed to weigh me down, I kept on grinding.

Then one afternoon I entered the apartment, to find DaDa alone lying on the couch. She was wearing a pair of sweatpants, white tube socks and a white tank top with no bra. When I walked through the living room I tried to move fast cuz I knew she probably watching the stories or Jerry Springer. Yet, I became more of her attention than whatever she had been watching.

"Ooh! Daddy I love to see you in that grey crushed linen suit. You haven't worn that in ages," she said.

"Yeah! Well we've got reservations at the W Hotel, downtown on 15ᵗʰ Street," I replied as I laid the plastic covered clothing on the back of a chair in the dining area.

"Wow! The elegant building that all the stars stay in?"

"Yes!"

"The one that allows its occupants to see the White House from their balconies and other landmarks and parts of the city? Daddy wait! That hotel has a bar and restaurant on the top floor that is so serious. Strictly five star material Daddy."

"Yeah! You sound a little like you done had your ass up in that spot before. Let me find out," I said as I walked over to couch and took a seat. I was wearing a pair of True Religion jeans and a black t-shirt, with some black Air Force Ones. DaDa scooted over and snuggled up under me. I kicked off my Nike's and sighed for a little relief.

"Before I started managing the girls and was out there caught up chasing niggas for change, I tricked and trimmed a few in there. It's absolutely beautiful Daddy. How is it that we have reservations in such a prestigious place?"

"I should be asking you that, however I got an email from the Chef, David Williams. He has become a big fan of the Ladies Club and has asked me to bring all of you for a night out."

"Is this business or pleasure?"

"DaDa it's always business but I figure that while we're racking in a good amount of bread, we can all get some pleasure up out of this event."

"Wow! It's obvious that we were thinking alike for a change. I have our passports and our IDs in my Gucci bag. The Italians at Sabiato's in Georgetown mentioned how they were sorry that they missed you and you should call whenever you could."

"Yeah! Well I am gonna miss Jimmy and Pauly, yet I ain't got no time to say no goodbyes." I said while walking over to the table to examine their work.

"That bag in the chair is from them also," said DaDa pointing.

I first examined our IDs and passports and admired the very intricate details. I ran my fingers over the plastic and wondered for a moment. The job was excellent. I couldn't do anything but smile. Then I reached down and grabbed a box and opened it.

"These will match my suit just fine and Wow! Pauly sent me a beautiful belt to match."

DaDa came over and peeped over my shoulder, "Is that snake skin or something?"

"Bitch! These things have been hand made out of elephant skin, with an ivory clasp on each shoe."

"I've never seen anything made out of elephant before. The buckle is made out of ivory too and it's so beautiful and it's definitely rare and different Daddy."

"Lil momma you're seeing a lot of things different now and you will Baby as long as you step out of the realm of your neighborhood, or any hood for that matter."

DaDa smiled at me and for what reasons I like to think were because I opened her eyes to an all new world. Or was it truly the other way around?

"Tonight is gonna be special DaDa so please make sure that the girls are all on their best behavior. Trick, trap and trim and play for every damn dollar tonight. The stakes are gonna be large and the sky is the limit."

"Daddy I got it."

"Good send that girl a text message to let her ass know that you will need her to drive yall around. As a matter of fact, take care of everything to rent a beautiful car for yall to pull up in. I will be riding in something different and I'll meet yall there."

September and Fire were both big fans of Facebook and they had both purchased pink Toshiba, Protégé, Ultra notebooks with some Hello Kitty designs. Nothing could keep them from checking on their friends or updating their pages. September bragged about having 3,063 friends. I wasn't amazed by it. I had only tried to convince her that not everybody should receive the title of a friend. She hadn't any real idea of who the hell she was meeting online.

Fire googled everything. If you said it, Fire would take the time out to pull it up on Google to research exactly what the hell it was. We got into a heated discussion about Solbiato and how it was a hell of a clothing line. She googled it and found out it was a gay Italian who invented the lavish stretch material and infamous style.

Candy and Labymba could care less about Facebook. Labymba bought an iPad but she only used it for an online course that she took in Child Care Development. Whenever engulfed in the slim, touch screen monitor, she would be heavily into her studies.

Candy played on her iPhone so much that it was if they were joined at the hip. She slept with the phone, ate with the phone, fucked with the phone and even took her baths texting in the water with it.

"Hit me on my Twitter page," she would say to end most of her conversation.

That night before we went out, I stood in the doorway and watched while all the girls fiddled with their computer gadgets. I stared at all of the while they were engulfed in modern technology, the new way of the world. A simple press of a button, a few taps of some keys or light tap on a touch screen monitor. All of these were ways to shop, to read, to learn, to view new ideas, new crafts and all sorts of new ways of living.

The world had advanced so much so that at any time, you could freeze the actual moment you were in and capture it all on film. Then with a click of a button, you could add a phrase and send it to someone directly with your phone.

Communication had changed so much that the US Postal Service had gone up on the price of stamps several times. All in an effort to encourage people to start writing again· Yet technology has us so engulfed in computer gadgets that there is a very slight chance it'll ever be like yesteryear·

The grocery stores are doing away with cashiers and are being run by self-checkout lanes· Applications for employment are done over the computer and replied back through your own personal email address· College and certain trades are taken at home now at the hands of your own personal device· Children text and keep up with each other and create more and more ways to set trend on the internet· To get caught would mean that I would love myself in time· I damn sure didn't want to lose and with my account now totaling $116,000 I began to focus all of my attention on escaping successfully·

The girls were high spirited and full of excitement· For some reason, they always seemed to be like that before they were about to go out· This evening, Mary J· Blige's latest CD was thumping loud throughout the apartment· They were singing, dancing, trying on clothes and moving fiercely· The apartment smelled like burnt hair, perfume and pussy· One by one they had gotten themselves together and were about to step out in class· They were sexually and emotionally empowered· Each possessing the fact that on this night, they were gonna get some major money by using the ultimate power of the pussy· Something men had grown weak to for ages·

Behind the sounds of the music, a horn honked loudly·

"Bommp! Bommmmmmppppppppp! Bommmmmppp!"

DaDa ran to the front window and lifted it eagerly· Then she smiled and yelled out into the street· "We'll be right down girl· Ooh! You look great!"

After the girls all left· I headed out myself· Here I was playing so damn hard in the GAME and hadn't treated myself· I grew tired of lying dead, playing scared but yet and still getting ahead· I left the apartment in a cab and went out for some me time·

Chapter 19

At Fullers Barber Shop on 12ᵗʰ Street, in South East, I jumped in the barber chair and got it straight to the white meat. I let the young dude shave me clean with a straight razor and work all around my goatee. I didn't even know the youngin but I let him hook me up and he did that. The job he did was so nice, I paid him twice. Then I took a look in the hand held mirror he held and admired myself. Clean.

I had set out to get fly, real quick, get in and get out that is. Yet, as I was leaving Fullers, I got sidetracked when I saw the incredibly large dice game going down in the back room on the floor. I walked into a rain game. There were a bunch of playa's getting down and throwing a set of dice around. They were shooting craps.

There was a pimp named Sophisticated P, from uptown off of 7ᵗʰ and T a big dude from the Maryland side who went by Big Kenny. A smooth hustla named Mississippi Charlie who swore he couldn't be beat. When I viewed that nigga Charlie up in there, I knew the game wasn't being played fair. Even Pimp La Smooth and Pretty Willie from off of Division Avenue were up in the spot. A rack of old fly ass gangstas.

A light skin cat that looked to be in his early thirties, low haircut, with some mean looking brown eyes, by the name of Dirty Redz was leaning on the back wall. When I first walked into the smoke filled area, I noticed him looking at my shoes.

"Damn Slim! You rocking the shit out of them joints."

"Thanks!" I said while I looked down and noticed his all black Prada boots that were scuffed up and show enough rugged.

"Yeah! I don't do animals but on my Momma, them joints is off the chain. I could jive like go for something like that."

"Oh yeah?"

"Yeah! You shooting?" he asked.

"For sure, what's up?"

"I'm cutting six and eights and I'm changing all money if anything come up in my Fathers shop, I'm gonna show enough straighten it."

"That's what's up. I'm good on the change Soldier and I can't do nothing but respect your G shit."

"Go ahead then Slim, get your bankroll right."

"OK Lil Daddy you got that."

I could see the imprint on his waist line. This nigga was surely packing something real big and had given me the impression that he wouldn't think twice about using it.

What made me feel good about getting down was these niggas weren't playing anywhere as good as they were looking. I myself had thrown on my grey crushed linen suit by Yves Saint Laurent (YSL). My left earlobe was weighed down with a single two carat diamond stud. My wrist was a little something nasty, a pearl oyster, black face, Rolex with a three carat matching Rolex ring. Just enough to catch the eye and make somebody blink a few times while they stared at the diamond encrusted bezel. My bone colored, silk shirt matched the ivory clasp on my loafers. I fit right in with the slacks, lizards and gators. Honestly, I didn't give a fuck about their gear. I was out to get these niggas for their bread.

There were Tear Tappers, Conners, Pigeon Droppers, Drag playas, Pick Pockets, Pimps, Creepers and even Noters for those who don't know, these were some of the Boss Ass Playas who would suit up and play for real high odds. Dressing the part that was sometimes needed for whatever move was necessary. Different games that required every individual to be a Boss in his own damn lane. Sometimes switching them so that they could continue to short con or run a decent long con game on their mark.

I side betted a few times and patiently waited my turn. When I first touched the dice, my hand was dead ass cold. I couldn't make point, lost a little and let the next nigga roll. Then by the time they came back around, them old playas thought I had lead on seven and eleven. I came out the gate bucking em hard. I hit a few six and eights. Hollered at Nina Ross and played the bar with the ten and four. Split my finger looking for the fish, all along snapping my fingers and talking cash shit.

After my luck ran good for so long and I was all the way up on game, I figured I was in the best situation to get gone. I stuffed and cuffed and played pretty good shooting a hundred, bet a hundred. The house man Dirty Redz had passed around a few bottles of Patron and I acknowledged the Playa on the way back out the door.

"Drinks on me this time. Here you go Soldier."

"Yeah! Be easy Slim," he said while accepting the small balled up wad of hundreds from my hand.

Just as I got to the door, Mississippi Charlie slid up on me, saying, "Damn

Playa! Shoot em up shooter. How lucky can you be?"

Yet I ain't never been stupid. That old nigga was trying to get me to shoot the bird up out the bush. Only a fool would've given him the chance to go heads up at my winnings. I had cracked for $7,200 I got a haircut, a few shots of Patron. I looked at him tight faced.

"Playa, I'm gone."

Chapter 20

My phone went off just as I got in a cab headed away from the spot. It was a text message from DaDa.

Daddy da girls n i r good can't wait 2 c u dress 2 impress cuz we have ur gonna luv da ladies club when u c it only wish we could've made our entrance 2gether I'm supposed 2 b on ur arm ttyl

True enough she was but in the event of treating myself, I felt the need to step up in that function like the Boss Playa that I am.

At 9:00 p.m. the ceremony to commemorate the Chef, David Williams was due to start. Several people arrived early to mingle and kick it. Valets were parking their cars as people made their grand entrances. Paparazzi were there and cameras flicked and flashed as appearances were made.

David Williams had cooked for a lot of prestigious people and had planned to announce his opening of a new untitled large chain of restaurants in the Metropolitan area. Everybody was there or soon would be there. The after party was where the girls would entertain several of the guests and Ballers and major playas of all walks of life. This was the spot to be on this Saturday evening.

Jay Fields an old time gangsta slid through that night and he looked real dapper Dan in a pair of brown Gucci loafers with a brown three piece suit. Took it back to the seventies and cocked a mean ass Fedora, ace duce on em. Gave the crowd a head nod and raised a diamond studded hand up in the air. Cameras flicked like crazy.

Mississippi Charlie had that Mississippi swag, cold killing the event. When his feet stepped out that Escalade truck, he was right. He wore a double breasted, two piece, beige suit. A burnt orange silk shirt and a pair of burnt orange ostrich had him walking real smooth like. He stopped in mid stride and a brown skin chick with real thick hips, short hair don't care, named Lameesa caught onto his arm. Her dress was fitting her ass some kind of special and it wasn't the matching colors that made it look so good. It was the split up her left side that gave the crowd a peak at a tattoo of a pair of dice that did it all. Not only could that old Playa shoot but that night, he was winning big.

My ladies were next. DaDa led the pack and she came down that entrance way with a scarlet re Cavalli pants suit on that made her look so expensive and so exquisite. The dynamic diva had a silver fox fur stole draped over her shoulders and a peak of cleavage teased in between. Tightly she gripped her iPad.

Following behind her in a plum colored asymmetrical neckline, ruffled gown, was Labymba. The dress was created by Tom Ford but even more than that, it was created to fit her body. With a low hem, you could see her toes painted a matching plum, as they stuck out of her six inch, peep toe design heels.

September was flawless and she looked stunning in a red one shoulder by Christian Dior. With her matching colored heels, she was well put together. September had a body that made those camera click and click and click. Vivacious was a word that didn't do her any justice. "Damn!" was overly expressed that evening.

Candy had gotten her wig on straight that damn night. It wasn't to curly or a hot pink to mimic Nikki Minaj. It was a golden brown and it hung just low enough to even look like it could've been her Donatella Versace. Candy wore six inch heels to match and just like a few of the other girls, her iPhone was tight within her grip.

Fire was last and she hit the entrance way like a fire ball. Her gown was by Christian Louboutin and it was black, yet trimmed in red. It was a strapless design that was accented with a fray of beads on the front. Fire was killing them and her Louboutin pumps, had see through heels that took her all the way over the top.

The night was absolutely spectacular and stars were lit up in the sky. The moon was full and although it had gotten rather cool in the night air, the light drizzle of rain couldn't destroy the atmosphere. I had enjoyed seeing the ladies and do believe me, I was impressed. They hadn't spotted me and I was only three cars behind them. Coincidentally we had all managed to arrive at close to the same time. As the traffic barely moved up for its occupants to make their grand entrances, my eyes noticed something crazy. I even shook my head real fast to make sure that I wasn't seeing things or that the few drinks I'd had weren't fucking with my mind. Then as the same 550 SL Benz that carried the Ladies Club exited to leave the entrance way. I noticed her behind the wheel of the car.

I whipped out of the line and immediately began to follow. This was absolutely unbelievable. She was driving slow at first and maneuvering through the downtown streets. I followed her with a few cars leading in front of me as she took the 4th Street Tunnel and hit I-295. I was fumbling, trying to light up a backwood to calm my nerves. She picked up speed was doing about 70 mph in the middle lane. After passing a South Capitol Street exit, up ahead she bared off to the right. I let her get at least a four car lead but I was trailing her carefully. A fool tried to cut me off and I put my foot heavy on the gas. She was speeding now and even more than that, she could drive.

I knew the city and even with the four car lead that she had, I knew she was headed for South East when she shot past the Nationals Stadium Exit an onto Martin Luther King Bridge. We flew over the funky ass Anacostia River. When she came off the bridge and took the Martin Luther King exit, she got stuck at the light. I rolled off the bridge and was one car behind her. She hadn't paid me any mind and I got a good look at her through her own rearview mirror. Comfortable with that, I followed as she made a left turn at the Big K liquor store and went up Morris Road. She wound up leading me to the Woodland Projects. There were people hanging out all over the hood and when she made the right into the first alley off of Bruce Place; I slowed for the large pothole.

She parked by the big green dumpster and as she front end dipped down and came back up, I noticed her cut her lights off. Two dirt bikes bounced up and onto the sidewalk and weaved around a few laundry poles, roaring loudly into the night. A group of young men wearing North Face jackets, hoodies and jeans stared at both cars as we entered that alley.

The ice cream truck that came through the alley behind me took the attention off of us. Kids seemed to come out of everywhere and rushed the truck. Several were barefoot, snotty nosed and toting a brother or sister along with them.

With the crushed linen suit on and the soft elephant skin shoes, I had only packed my pearl handle twenty two revolver, something small enough to conceal in my pocket. I grabbed it out of the glove compartment and quickly exited the car in the drizzling rain.

She hadn't gotten out of the Benz yet, and seemed to be counting some money as she sat behind the wheel. As soon as her feet hit the raggedy ass parking lot pavement, I met April's face with the hardest smack I could muster.

"OH GOD!" She screamed as she bent and covered for any more unsuspected blows.

"Shut up Bitch! I ought to kill you."

I hawk spit on her and violently kicked at her. Yet she moved out of the way quickly.

"Hey! Hey! Bae wait a minute. I can explain." She pleaded.

"You sorry good for nothing Bitch! What the fuck you mean you can explain? You ran off with my money and left me for dead."

When she went to speak again, I smacked her and saw blood squirt up out of her mouth. Then I grabbed her and began to choke her so viciously. As I squeezed her tightly around her throat, I could see my mother's face. As the rain fell, I continued to choke her and I saw a casket being dropped into the ground. Tears were streaming down my cheeks and beads of sweat were on my forehead and my brow, mixed with the rain.

I missed being able to say any last words to my Mother. I never got to see her smile again. In my mind, I could only remember how she had spoken of getting her hair permed and pressed with a hot comb, so she could look good. Momma wanted to see me before it was over. Momma knew that she was about to go.

There are no do overs in life and I missed not just a golden opportunity but a platinum one. I continued to choke April and my strength had made me pick her up off her feet. As I cried and squeezed her throat, her feet began to move frantically and her face started to turn a pale blue. I was crying harder than I had since the last phone call, with my mother.

Then instantly, I was struck from behind with a devastating blow. The first one made me release April from the death grip I had on her. The second knocked me totally unconscious. She fell down on the wet pavement, with me following directly behind her. Yet, when I awoke, I wasn't in the parking lot amongst the broken glass, pot holes or crack and weed bags. I was lying on a couch with an ice pack on the coffee table in front of me. Then as I struggled to regain my vision, faintly I heard footsteps on the hallway stairs.

"Hey! Spider I'm glad to see that you're alright Soldier."

"Cory, damn is that you?" I questioned after I had rubbed my eyes good.

"You better believe it," he said. "Your cousin Pooh took April up out of here to try and soothe her nigga. She was shaken all the fuck up."

"Damn! Your dreads have gotten long as shit nigga. Your tall geek looking ass need to tell me who the fuck? Or how the fuck a nigga slid up on me and got at me."

"You zapped out Slim and was launching for real. Everybody around here had started to come outside and if I hadn't knocked you the fuck out, the Feds would've show enough did something with you. Yeah! Cuz you damn sure was about to kill shorty ass."

"So, you hit me huh? I questioned.

"Yeah! Nigga cut the bullshit. Don't start that faking shit with me. Let's say that's a little get from that fight we had way back in 2000 on New Year's Day."

I cracked a smile and Cory did too. He sat down on the reclining chair.

"Yeah! I remember that nigga. Pour me a fucking drink. I know Pooh got something up in here."

"They gonna swing by the 51 liquor store on their way back and fucking with your cousin crazy ass, she gonna scoop up some Remy."

"That's what's up," I said as I sat up.

"Just don't launch out nigga. Hear the girl out. I know damn well you fucked up about your mother. We all were. Wanda kept lil Cory and Kenya and she was there whenever we needed her. Shit! That couch you sitting on was your mothers. We got it out the house after the funeral."

I looked down at the beige upholstery with the floral print and although I cracked a slight smile. A tear streamed down my face. I leaned my head back and I pictured her smile. Cory had definitely been right. Mommas were there for everybody and although she never had much, she gave out to whomever needed. She would cook sometimes and feed other kids on the block. When I was pumping and bumping, momma would let me and my lil homeys eat. Or whenever they would be running from the man, she would open the side door for them to have a place to hide.

When the back door opened both Cory and I turned to look, Pooh walked in wearing a scarf and some jeans and a Be Be t-shirt and slippers. April came in behind her with her head down. I hadn't paid attention to how well she was dressed. Her pants suit was black and her heels were Gucci. Her cleavage was showing a little and the pants hugged her hips tightly.

I eyed Pooh and immediately, I saw the family resemblance so well, the small pointy nose, the little black moles, the high cheek bones and the eyes. I saw momma in the way that she moved towards me. What I saw was not just the same brown skin complexion but another child that my mother had raised.

"Hey Boy!" Pooh exclaimed· "I'm sure glad as hell you crazy ass is alright· You know better than that bullshit· Tighten up!"

She handed me a black plastic bag and afterwards her and April just stood in the doorway to the living room·

"Thank you," I said·

"Yeah! Well, get you a couple of sips and get out of here·"

"What's up?" I questioned while looking puzzled·

"You and April need to move fast cuz· The Feds are supposedly hot on your trail· I don't know what the hell you've done this time · · ·"

"Hold up!" I shouted·

"No you hold up," said Pooh· "They have been to your father's house, you sons house and they have been asking questions around the city· I ain't talking about the warrant squad either boy· I'm talking about the FBI·"

I got the drift real quick and immediately, I put my shoes on and stood up· Then I reached in the bag and retrieved a bottle of Hennessy Black instead of the usual Remy Martin· I poured myself two quick shots into one plastic cup and downed it·

"Whatever the differences yall have, love conquers all· Work that shit out· I love yall," said Pooh·

"Yeah! Get it right Spider," said Cory·

He stood up and gave me a solid five and a real tight hug· After that he handed me my gun· I looked at him a little funny and stuck it in my waist line· Me and April headed out the back door· Pooh stood in the doorway with the porch light on·

"I'm driving Spider," said April·

I looked directly in her brown eyes and at that moment, there wasn't any need for words· I turned back towards the door of Pooh's house·

"Hey!" I screamed as I dug into my pocket· "Take these don't say I ain't never give you nothing·

The title is in the glove compartment. I love you Cuz."

Pooh caught the keys to the 1987 Cadillac Seville and smiled real big like. I had used my winnings in the crap game to snatch up the whip from an older dude on Morris Road. I believe Pooh may have still been standing there as we dipped in and around a few of those potholes and sped up out of that parking lot.

Chapter 21

We rode in complete silence for a while. April hadn't even cut he radio on. It was an irritable silence and after a few minutes, I spoke, "I need to go to my house."

April whipped the car over on an unknown street, "No! What you need to do is listen to me for a minute," she said as she had both of her hands on the steering wheel and her head rested on them.

I remained quiet for a little while and figured I owed her that much. I definitely wanted to hear just what the hell she had to say. When April looked up and over me, there were tears in her eyes that formed but had not fallen.

"Spider, I know that I walked away from you at a very crucial time in your life. Damn it! I know I did. Yet, you are so selfish and so self-centered that you don't care about anybody else's feelings but your fucking own."

April pounded the steering wheel several times with anger then she continued, "While you were in that jail, I was out here with your mother. I spoke to her on the phone regularly before she passed. At that time, I was your woman, your partner and I have always been your friend. Your mother was so sick. She had begun to eat plates smaller than what a woman feeds her child. Her digestive system wasn't allowing her to eat certain foods. Not all the time could she throw back up either? Sometimes, her bowels would become so bloated. The complications varied daily. Then suddenly, her liver began to fail.

"What?"

"I know you didn't know about that part. Nobody wanted to tell you. Hell, I'm sorry that I kept it from you. I realize now that regardless of the situation, a man has got a right to know about the ones he loves, even if he is in prison or jail."

"You damn right!" I exclaimed.

April sniffled and then cleared her throat. "People become afraid of what one might do and don't want the men in those situations to make them any worse."

"That shouldn't matter," I responded. "They should always have a right to know."

"Well anyway, it got bad Bae. So bad that blood was not properly flowing through her body. She turned very dark and she was hurting so badly. Her feet swollen up and even if your mother wanted to, there is no way in hell she could've walked down that long ass hallway to see you."

"For real?"

"Yes! For real Spider. Your mother was taking Morphine because the pain was so damn bad. She was hurting, I was hurting. Stomach cancer hurt the entire family deeply."

Tears began to flow heavily down both of our faces as we sat in that car. The pain was more than evident. The pain was real and it could only be measured by an abyss.

Together, we let out our hurt. Together we grieved in that Mercedes Benz and sniffled a little as the engine hummed. The glow from a street light shined down on the dash board and the very reflection of that light let me see her. April was being truthful and I couldn't hate her or be mad at her for that. I could see the pain in her eyes. I knew that she hurt and the same pain was now embedded in her soul.

"I'm sure you still wanna know what happened or why I even disappeared."

"Yes! I do." I responded with a stern but raspy voice.

"Spider I nutted up and honestly, I just couldn't do it."

"You couldn't do what?" I asked.

"I couldn't go see her or go get her, or even go do her hair. I as already too damn emotional Spider. There I was wondering if I was gonna lose you to prison for only God knows how long and I was a hot mess. Then your mother was expecting me to do so very much."

"And?"

"And, I cracked up and started getting high," said April as she began to cry again.

"What?" I questioned while straining to see her.

"Yeah! I started popping pills and got all the way out there."

"You were gone like that?"

"On the day I was supposed to go get your mother, I had actually been in a coma like sleep."

"What the fuck? Sleep? How the hell were you sleep?"

"I had been up for three days straight rolling. I went to work and even bounced around afterwards a little too much."

A car pulled alongside of us slow, driving in the opposite direction. It was apparently looking for somebody or an address on the very same street where we sat. It passed us and right after began honking its horn a few times. Then a young dude in a North Face jacket, Nike boots and jeans, exited a house. He ran off the porch and got into the car and the cab pulled away from the curb slowly. The red tail lights disappeared in my side view mirror.

"I began to medicate my pain Spider. I didn't know that they were gonna take me so far. I hadn't any idea that I would lose control of my life."

"Bitch! You still don't have control of your life. You went to the projects trying to cop some pills tonight and I ain't green."

"Those pills are what has been fueling your exotic Ladies Club shit. Those pills are what have had your girls out there willing to work so damn hard. I've got enough control to know that you ain't the smartest nigga in the world."

"What the hell you talking about?" I asked curiously.

"You put a lot of trust into that dyke ass bitch DaDa."

"How do you figure that?"

"I've been driving those girls around for a long ass time now. Long enough to know that she don't love you and she could never be loyal to you."

"Sounds a little bit like you're hating to me. Are you mad because she is taking your place?" I asked with a devilish grin.

"I'm more mad that she's sleeping with Fire and those two bitches have been deceiving you in your face."

"What? You're tripping." I said a little irritated.

April took a sip from a Rock Creek grape soda she had sitting in the cup holder and sat the bottle in between her legs. She turned towards me, "No!" She said. "I'm telling you what I know. DaDa likes pussy. That's the reason she never fucks on dates, she dances. She would always prefer that her and Candy perform at every bachelor party. I would watch her and she could really move."

I adjusted my seat to sit up fully. "Fuck her dancing" I yelled. "This ain't about how the hell she could move," I said with anger.

"Your right and I want you to know that it's never really been about you. Somehow you thought you were being slicker than a jar of KY Jelly. You obviously hadn't noticed either. You weren't the one who got Candy out the club, DaDa did."

"How the hell did you know that?"

"I know that and I knew that you would find me. I've never stopped knowing that you love me Spider. We are one and I owe you for life. So, let me be the Boss ass Bitch that I am and help you get your life right. I have always needed to be the woman that needed to be on your arm. I know that we need to shoot back downtown and make our entrance together."

"April it might be too late for that baby. Everybody has probably already showed up."

"It ain't too late for us to attend the function or to repair everything we've built," she said and then leaned over to kiss me.

I could taste the tears on her lips. It was a kiss that was salty yet so sweet. I ran my fingers through her hair and cupped her chin with the other. It had been so long since I tasted love, since I tasted the truth. I continued to kiss April for as long as she let me, we fogged up the windows in the car.

Chapter 22

On our way back downtown, we pulled into a gas station and it was crowded with cars and pedestrians. April and I were at an Exxon, a few blocks away from the "D" Street tunnel. I stepped out of the beautiful automobile very carefully, not wanting to damage my shoes at all. As I began to take the knob off the gas tank, I watched April exit the passenger side.

Her hips swayed and I stared at her walk that distinctive walk of hers. Then that was suddenly interrupted. Not one but two Capitol State Police patrol cars pulled into the parking lot. Immediately, I put my head down and turned towards the machine over the pumps.

I had gotten my picture on my bank card. The Bank of America offered several different designs and I preferred to see my damn self getting money. So, after I admired my face on plastic real quick, I slid it into the machine and typed in my pin number and payment selection. Unexpectedly, my card was declined. I wiped the card off with a blue towel that I retrieved from the dispenser over the windshield wipers. Then I reinserted it into the machine. It read the exact same thing, DECLINED.

At first the two patrol cars parked side by side as the drivers looked to be carrying on a conversation. Then one of them pulled out of the parking lot and the other whipped the car along the opposite side of the tank. I couldn't get the gas cap on fast enough. Before I could get in the car, the officer spoke.

"Good evening Sir."

"Good evening," I replied but still avoiding eye contact.

My heart was racing and I didn't wanna seem like I was in any way shape or form running from the law. So reluctantly, I made conversation by asking, "Would you happen to know how I can get to the MCI Center from here?"

I looked up in the face of a young black cop, brown skin and glasses. His badge read Bennet Napoleon.

"Sir, did you say the MCI Center?" he questioned.

"It's OK honey," said April, walking up from behind me. "The station manager was nice enough to write them down for us. Hello officer," she stated as she turned towards him and gave a sassy look and smile.

He grinned, "Hello mam. I am glad that you two have been helped. The Wizards are playing the Clippers tonight and I expect the Wizards to come through but who am I?" He asked with a smile.

I smiled back and me and April both got in the car. I still wanted to seem like I was legit, so I had April put her window down halfway. I leaned over her little and spoke, in a loud voice.

"Thanks!" I said. "I do know that when a team plays hard it'll sometimes go beyond the call of duty. Victory is something we all want to obtain. No matter the fouls, continuing to play through any adversities is the main goal. I don't know who'll win tonight officer but I do know that somebody will win."

"Well you two enjoy your night and I will try and enjoy mine. I'll ride down 7th Street and catch a few sneak peeks from the large screens that show a few highlights in front of the building. I've just started my shift and that's as close as I'll get. Goodnight and enjoy yourselves in Chinatown."

"Goodnight," I said and put my window up and pulled out of the parking lot.

The funny part about it was; I never got one drop of gas. Me and April got up out of there with the quickness. By the time we made it back downtown to the W Hotel, the commencement part of the ceremony was over and the dinner party had ended. Everyone was now engulfed in the atmosphere of a Ball or much more of an elegant party.

The music was beating through the huge speakers. It was old funk. When we entered the room, Mary Jane by Rick James was roaring and thumping loudly. The sounds vibrated off the huge cathedral ceilings. Lovely, golden colored chandeliers hung and sparkled. Their crystal covered lights, shimmered with a tremendous light. Each table had an array of candles in the middle and golden colored table cloths. The sterling silverware was still in its place at our own table and our chairs looked as if they had never been moved.

Me and April didn't sit down. We went straight to the dance floor and started a mean ass two step. April still had moves and she knew what to do out on that floor. Rick James sang and we stepped and hopped to the beat. In the midst of our groove, I looked up and noticed more than enough faces amongst the many.

September was enjoying herself and so was the white guy that she was with. Whoever he was, he had lots of class. He was dunned in a black linen suit with a cream silk shirt and some crème colored square toe shoes. Pretty fly for a white guy. I never knew who he was or what he might've owned. Yet, with September on his arm, I knew that she was destined to tap into his bank roll.

I saw Drina and Aaron Lancaster, a married couple who owned a couple of Carvel Ice Cream Stores in the Metropolitan area. They had a beautiful vacation spot that they would rent out to me and the girls in West Virginia. A place we used to escape at times. Aaron and Drina were both dressed spectacular and enjoying the evening.

Mississippi Charlie was spinning his lady friend all around and they were getting funky and getting down. She smiled back at that old fella while they moved like two old swans.

Trickya, a real South East nigga who shocked a many had been spotted on the dance floor with his wife Falomeena. She had to be the one to convince him to put on some clothes cuz he was never into anything other than Nike boots, jeans and Black Label or True Religion. Falomeena looked down at him as he moved and grooved with his arm wrapped tight around one of his most prize possessions. The other had to be his 1969 Fleetwood Cadillac that he rode around the city in using as a sex machine.

I caught an eye full of a real light complexion female that I thought was in the hallway with me when I first met DaDa. Only I wasn't sure because her feet looked a little big and with the scarf tied around her neck so tight. I was hoping she could breathe. A rather husky older gentleman was holding onto shim for dear life. Someone should've told him that you can't slow dance to a fast song.

We danced to about two or three more songs and I decided to get some punch out of the huge punch bowl off to the left of the dance floor. April went and sat down and while I was getting us both some of the pineapple filled beverage, somebody slid up behind me.

"Hey Sexy Daddy! Where I'm from, we ride on elephants to get to where we need to be. You so bad that you wear them on your feet and carry the elephant and its ivory like a cold G.

I could smell her alluring perfume and I loved its sweet flavor. She was so close that I could feel her warm breath on my neck. Without turning around, I shot back, "Bitch! If I'm that bad then put it in my pocket and show me that even in this space age era we can sell your good pussy and keep getting ahead."

I felt her hand slide into my pocket and instead of dropping something in it; she fiddled around until she felt my dick. After a good grasp of what she wanted, she let go and then spoke.

"I transferred $5000 in between the two account numbers that you told me to. I did everything online Daddy. I have a gentleman who is taking me to Florida for the weekend."

"My pocket is deeper than that Bitch!" I replied.

"It's only half now and I will get the rest once I get to his yacht. Which is docked in Miami, Florida at one of their piers.

"OK."

"Besides," Labymba said as she stepped around and turned to face me. As beautiful as she was, I just stared while she continued, "You should know that for you Daddy and to get my education right, I am gonna make sure that the numbers are to your liking every time. I want to learn very much and receive many degrees so that my family will be proud of me one day."

Staring into her eyes was tricky; Labymba had the ability to capture a man within the grips of her seductive stare. I diverted my eyes to her flawless dark skin and noticed that she had a gold glitter, flickering on her skin.

"True enough," I said. "The last account is towards your studies for sure. I told you that I got you and Labymba, I meant that."

She smiled and then in an instance, her facial expression changed that quick. "DaDa must got me," she said. "She's been online all evening making some form of transactions with the Bank of America also."

"There is no way that has anything to do with you or I and either of those accounts."

"How do you figure?" asked Labymba with a raised brow.

I responded quickly, "I never gave her either of those account numbers for any reason at all."

"Nor have I," she stated coldly.

Another song came on blaring loud from the speakers. "Money! Money! Money! Some people really need it. Hey! Hey! Do thangs. Do thangs. Do bad thangs with it."

As I listened to the classic by the OJs, I looked up and noticed that September and her date made way to the elevator. The inside of those human carriages were magnificent and donned with brass railings, mirrors and fixtures. The number 9 lit up and the doors closed as their playful cuddling faded in between the small gap.

Chapter 23

As the night went on, me and April got back out on the dance floor and dipped a little more. We got into another mean ass two step and were enjoying ourselves while we danced and grooved. I strained my eyes through the fly suits, slacks and fashionable gowns and dresses. I was trying so hard to spot DaDa in the midst of the event.

Candy was setting up in a far corner. She had an older cat damn near drooling on himself; while she looked so stunning in that white strapless gown she wore. To see Candy with a man meant that she was working and working hard at winning. Candy was famous with scheming up on a way to get a trick to spend and usually they would spend real big.

The guy Candy was with looked to be in his early forties. He had on a black two piece suit with a wide brimmed hat, some thick ass glasses and a bow tie and suspenders. Looking like one pure Hot Bamma with much money to blow.

The spiked up punch just wasn't doing it for me to much anymore. I caught one of the cocktail waitresses and ordered a bottle of Rose and an apple martini for April. She seemed to be having just as much fun as I was. We grabbed a seat at our reserved table and while we were sipping and getting a kick out of watching other people dance. I noticed some peculiar movement. I didn't make notice to April. Yet it was extremely obvious that something was going on somewhere else in the Hotel.

Security had come into the extravagant ballroom and whispered in not one but a few of the staff ears attending the function. Some of their facial expressions clearly showed that whatever news they were getting wasn't anything good at all. There was quite a bit of movement by the door and all of it was being done by either hotel security or other staff.

Then I spotted something a little more irregular than that. Two wide shouldered white men in grey suits. The both of them were clean shaven and definitely not looking to party. They had come inside of the entrance door and stopped right there. Apparently, they were looking around for someone.

April noticed how she had lost my attention. So, she followed my eyes and then turned slowly in her seat towards the door. After she turned back to me, she spoke.

"Damn Daddy! That doesn't look too good."

"You telling me," I responded.

"Those are the pigs and we need to cut all this short."

"April go get the car and meet me out front. Text that Bitch DaDa one more damn time. If I don't meet you out front within twenty minutes, then get the fuck on."

As April got up and headed for the door. I saw the two white men split up and disperse within the same very room that I was in. Then two more gentlemen, one an oriental and the other a black man, took their spots at the door. I knew damn well that

I couldn't sit there for too much longer. I got up and got on the dance floor. Instead of drawing a tip by running or moving fast, I danced through the crowd. I was spinning and jiving towards the fire exit door.

Then just as soon as I got ready to make my move towards it, I saw one of the wide shouldered white men stand directly in front of that exit. Quickly, I turned and dipped, sliding my feet back across the dance floor in the opposite direction. I had to get the hell up out of there and I wasn't gonna do it by spinning around in circles.

I noticed Candy and the older gentleman she was with. They were dancing but from the looks of it, she was leading him. He had clearly had too many drinks. I slid up on them and tapped the funny looking guy on his shoulder.

"Excuse me Sir, would you mind if I had one dance with the fine lady?" I asked.

"Sure, just understand that she's my main squeeze partner and she ain't leaving here with nobody but me," he stuttered.

"No problem Sir. I only want one dance."

"Little momma I'll be sitting right over there," he said while pointing in the direction of his table.

"OK Barthalamuel. I'll come jump in your arms after this song. Leave your hat on my head, you sexy man you."

That is exactly what he did, left me and Candy right there dancing. The trick had absolutely no clue. All he was thinking about was getting his freak on. There was no doubt that he would desire that more than anything else.

Candy looked up into my eyes and with her small hands on my waist, she spoke. "Spider come on Daddy. I'm gonna get you up outta here. Put on this hat and here," she said while she handed me a small pair of Adrian Ventidinni, personality glasses.

I followed Candy and sure enough she got me out of the ballroom and down one of the hallways. We took a door that read, STAIRS. When we opened the door a hotel security officer was coming out and had stopped us from using the stairwell exit.

"Hey! You can't go that way. There has been a murder and a young lady was strangled to death tonight."

"Wow!" I said in astonishment.

"That's crazy. Was it a black girl?" Candy asked.

"Mam," said the officer. "I can't go into details about that, but what I can do is make sure that you two get to a much safer part of this hotel."

So we followed the big brown skinned, wavy haired fellow up one hallway. He got a call over his radio and directed us to go up another long hallway. Only Candy spotted two police first and she instinctively pushed me into a doorway that also read, STAIRS. She had become a beautiful distraction and apparently neither one of those officers saw my face.

Chapter 24

I made it out on the streets of downtown DC I was drunk, cold and headed I don't know where real fast. I had stained my suit and lost my diamond studded earring, even scuffed my imported, elephant skin shoes. I looked down at my watch and noticed that it was 2:26 a.m. At that time in the morning, traffic was slow. Along with a few Metro buses that ran by the hour, there were newspaper delivery guys filling the street corner machines. The downtown area belonged to so many of the vagabonds and homeless people. They made refuge on park benches, laid on open grates and some aligned certain sections of the sidewalks.

Capitol State Police had barricades in front of every United States government building, along with at least two armed men. Capitol State Police cruised up and down every main street in marked patrol cars, anticipating any attempts on a government building.

As my drunkenness began to wear down, I had found myself walking on Constitution Avenue. For the longest, I had just been walking and walking. Then when I got to a light on 12th and Constitution Avenue, I stopped to cross the Street· A 1988, candy apple red, Eldorado with some chrome rims and smacked out tint pulled to the curb in front of me· It was definitely surprising· So, I dipped down to see who I could see·

As the car idled, the window began to crack slowly· Then the door cracked open and one foot came out the door and rest on the ashy ass pavement· I looked down and noticed that whoever it was, had on an Ostrich skin house slipper· I looked back up at him and noticed his silk scarf· You could see his permed out hair rolled up in some pink rollers that were barely sticking out of the fine silk material·

"Damn pimping! What's happening?"

"Stay Down, what's good?" I asked·

"Mr· Stay Down·"

"You got that· What's up with you?"

He looked me over as if he needed to be asking me the same damn question· "Look here," he said· "Baby pimping is sure enough good out here on these streets· You done went a little too far off into space· I've got that girl Sassafraz, Yankee, Moet and Genet and pimping you ain't seen nothing yet·"

In spite of me being a little cold, I couldn't be a hater· I've always been a congratulator· So, I shot back quickly, "Work dirt work· Get your money how you live· Pimping recognize true pimping·"

At that time he began to wrestle around in his pocket and pulled up a humongous bankroll of cash· Instead of handing me one of the one hundred dollar bills on the outside of the roll, he flipped it open to the middle and said, "We gonna ride my nigga before long, here·"

He handed me five crispy one dollar bills· I noticed his oversized diamond pinky ring, shining when I reached out for the money·

"It's up to you as a playa to turn your kibbles and bits into hunks and chunks·"

Before I could respond to that, he snatched his foot back in that pretty Caddy. He gave the horn a few toots and sped off leaving me standing in the bitter cold. I could see my breath in the air and I was frustrated and walking again. The streets ain't never loved anybody. The realest part of the GAME is you could be up one day and something could happen and you would be down the next.

I reached into my pocket and pulled out my iPhone. When I hit the power button, the screen came on, then it read, BATTERY and made an awful sound and died just that fast. I was going through it. I was looking a little rough but not bad enough to the point where I couldn't hale a Taxi. After several attempts, I finally flagged one down.

"Good evening Sir. Can you please take me to 202 Bruce Place in South East?"

Before the little Arab man could respond, he locked the doors with the power locks. Then he turned around in his seat and looked at me through the glass partition.

"You got money?" he asked.

"Yes! I have money Sir."

"Well I need a twenty dollar deposit and I will not move until I get it. If you don't like it, you can get out right here, right now."

"OK no problem," I responded.

He accepted a single twenty that I had and the crispy one dollar bills through the Plexiglas partition. Afterwards, he pulled away from the curb headed for South East. I had given him everything that I had in my pocket. Cash is so played out and not too many people walk around with it in their pockets any longer. Yet, my credit card seemed not to be working.

With so much racing through my mind, I laid my head back on the headrest to gather together my thoughts. I couldn't figure out how or even why there would be not one but several plain clothes officers at that function and looking for me. Or so I thought anyway.

I tried very hard to determine if at any time I did anything stupid or whether one of the girls had acted foolishly. Nothing came to mind. Then I even wrestled with DaDa and couldn't quite figure out where the hell she disappeared to. If she had set up a date to trick and trim a fella for some bread, she wouldn't have made me aware of it. She would've done just like any other one of the girls and went and handled her business. So, in my mind, that's where the hell she was.

I looked up and out of the front window of the cab and had noticed that the driver was bearing off to the right and taking an exit off of I-295 that read, *Pennsylvania Avenue*. Within minutes, I would be back in Woodland. I had figured that to be the safest place for me and I could rest there, get myself together and try and figure out my next damn move.

The cab driver went up Naylor Road, crossed Good Hope Road and turned onto Alabama Avenue. We passed Staton Elementary School then made a right onto Anger Place. That's when I told him to stop. I looked down at the end of the block and there were police all over the entrance way to the first alley. Several cars were parked along Bruce Place as well. The cab driver bent then looked up out of the front window and made me notice the helicopter circling in the sky above us. Without me saying anything, he whipped the cab around, got lucky, caught the light and made a quick left back onto Alabama Avenue.

How much more bad could my luck get? I was in between a rock and a hard place. I had the driver let me out at the BP gas station on Naylor Road. A spot that most people called, *Top of the Hill*.

The driver turned in his seat and spoke, "You owe me an additional $10 so that makes the total $35."

There wasn't no need for me to try and dig into my pocket for any more money. He had surely gotten the last of it. I stared back at the out of towner then yelled through the glass, "I gotta tell you like Nappy Head told Nappy China. I'm fucked up Slim and I done gave you my last damn ends. I'm broke, I'm done. It's been fun but I'm fucked up and I gotta run."

He made a terrible look and shot back, "You mean to tell me you had me bring you all this way and you ain't got no money?" he asked with disgust.

"Exactly." I responded plainly.

"Get your broke ass up outta my cab, you jive turkey."

Chapter 25

At 4:16 a.m. in the morning, I was stuck. Once the cab sped up out of the parking lot, I was left dead ass broke, without any power to activate my phone and only had enough change in my pocket to make one phone call. Anybody passing by would've thought I was a smoker out on a late night, straight geeking, looking for some boulders.

I managed to make a call to the one person that I knew would come through for me, no matter what. I hadn't wanted too but at that point I was down on my luck. He answered the phone on the fifth ring and in a raspy voice. We spoke briefly and I hung up believing that he would be there soon.

Sure enough, a black Suburban pulled into the parking lot thirty minutes later. He whipped around until he saw me standing in front of the pay phone. I could see the disturbed ass look on his face and his dismangled dreads through the untinted glass. In spite of, I jumped in on the passenger side and after I got in the truck, neither one of us said a word for a few minutes. He gave me some time to absorb the heat, so I soaked it up.

"You done lost your mind, I see."

"I wouldn't necessarily say that," I said without looking over at him.

"Why is it that you keep forgetting that I was a nigga caught up in those streets at one point and time? I played all those damn games. I grew up in the Eastgate Projects son."

"Yeah! I hear you."

"You hear me Asim but you don't understand me. I've told you that the number one rule to the GAME is, THE GAME IS NOT A GAME!"

"You say that like you play as hard as I do."

"That is my point exactly, you out there playing, when you should be taking your own damn life serious Son."

"I hear you, Pop." I responded.

Quickly, we both eyed one another, while our words penetrated each other deeply. Then he questioned, "So, you a pimp now huh?"

"Come on Pop."

"You a broke ass pimp, with no damn Cadillac."

I was heated and I looked over at my father and he was grinning but never took his eyes off the road. "Yeah!" he said. "You know what the hell a pimp will do when a hoe can't get that money don't you Son?"

"Hold the fuck up!" I screamed out while swinging over at him.

"Watch your damn mouth!" he shot back as he blocked my swing and swerved, then quickly regained control of the steering wheel.

"I don't know where the hell you think I'm taking you," he continued.

I looked out of the window and noticed that we were headed back towards the downtown area. With disgust I said, "You could've took me to the house."

"Son you can't stay there and until you get your stuff straight. I don't want you back there."

"Oh yeah!"

"Yeah! You done had all those polices banging on my door in the wee hours of the morning, waking up my woman and disturbing my home."

"Have they been to the house Pop?"

"Now you're going deaf. They've been there twice already and you need to go ahead and turn yourself in. I don't know what the hell you are running from, running ain't gonna make it no damn easier."

"Just exactly where were you planning on taking me downtown?" I asked while glancing over at him with a puzzled look on my face.

"There is a bag on the back seat with a pair of your sneakers and a few outfits that I got out of the basement."

"And."

"And, I'm taking you to Union Station. You can make your mind up there and they've got quite a few trains that will take your ass anywhere you wanna go."

"So, you just gonna kick me to the curb like that?"

"Son, you can miss me with that. I'm even gonna give you a couple of dollars and I shouldn't be doing that. You got me going down here in the middle of all this mess."

"What mess?"

"I've gotta take the "D" Street tunnel because they've got a lot of the streets downtown blocked off."

"For what?" I asked.

"Apparently, a young teenage girl was found tied up, her mouth was gagged and her throat had been slit."

"Damn how young was she?" I asked.

"I believe they say she was nineteen."

"Where did all this happen at?"

"At the W Hotel and whoever the sick dude was, apparently had raped her. It's been all over the news. Said the girl was dressed up real nice and they believe she was an escort or something. If you weren't running the streets all night, you would've known."

Before long, we pulled around the circle entranceway in the front of Union Station. An area where people were dropped off, picked up or either caught taxis. At 4:36 a.m. the flow of traffic to and from work or in and out of town. Pigeons littered the statues that sat in front of the large building. Several of the homeless had stood in areas around the building entrance, they panhandled several of the patrons.

As we eased around towards the entrance, I looked over at my father. He spoke with sincerity, "Son, I spent fourteen years and eight months of my life in the Feds. That was a substantial amount of time to be missing out of your life. I wasn't there for you growing up and son I am so sorry for that. I am sorry that I have not been the best damn Father that I could possibly be. My life was hard too son. I grew up in those raggedy projects in South East. Dudes in my hood were beefing with dudes who lived within the same damn project area. The top of the hill was beefing with the bottom of the hill. Jamaicans and New Yorkers were trying to take over with the drug trade. Crack and PCP were being introduced at an all-time high. Yet, they were being sent home in a countless amount of body bags. Plenty of those out of towners were being killed.

Son, my father, Mr. Wonderful was into gambling and women and he never had time for me. Yet, with all of the drama and drugs being sold around me, I tried to find a way out. My mother worked at the recreation center for sixteen years. That place couldn't serve as a safe haven for me after too long.

Look! I am a Muslim now and I made my mistakes and I'm not acting like my upbringing was an excuse for me to sell water. I received my punishment for manufacturing PCP and I've paid my debt to society. Listen to me son and don't go back down the road that I went down."

"I'm listening to you Pop," I said reluctantly.

He reached into his back pocket and retrieved his wallet. Then he looked over at me and paused for a second. "Here," Pop said while opening his bill fold. "Take this and be safe son. I've given you my best advice as a father. Running ain't gonna solve nothing. If you know best, you'll get out of those streets."

He pulled the truck up some more and I stuffed the money into my pocket, without counting it. I reached in the back and grabbed the bag that Pop had packed. Then I leaned over real quick and kissed the old man on his face. He abruptly snatched away.

"Get out of my truck Boy!" Pop screamed.

With a grin on my face, I jumped out of the truck and he hit the horn and pulled away from the curb.

Chapter 26

The heat inside of Union Station was circulating real good like. I hadn't been inside the huge building in years. At one time, there was a movie theater in the basement that served as one hell of a spot to take a lady. There were also several types of eateries and restaurant on the bottom floor.

Coming up the escalator, you could see a large Barnes and Nobles Book Store. On that same middle floor that I walked in on, is where people boarded and exited their trains. The ticket counters were in the middle of this mall. While waiting in line, you could glance up and see a few of the various boutiques and shops.

The third floor was accessed by stairs, leading to several of those same shops. Anyone coming in or leaving the city had a very wide variety of choices to choose an outfit, shoes, accessories or a meal from.

It was quite early still in the morning and I had been ripping and running so much that I hadn't sat down to eat good. Right across from the Barnes and Nobles, sat an open area Café' that I hadn't read the name of. I had seen a few patrons sipping on steamy cups of coffee and I figured that to be a better place than any.

I sat down in a booth and ordered a Mocha Latte and two slices of cheesecake. Without even counting the money that I had gotten from Pop, I assumed it to be enough to grab myself a little breakfast. After I ordered, I dug into my pocket and quickly counted the few bills that I had and I smile. He had given me $300 in a various amount of bills.

While waiting on the waitress to return, I ran over to the bookstore and grabbed myself a Washington Post Newspaper. Back at my table in a dash, I sipped on the Mocha Latte and devoured the first slice of cheesecake. Then I wiped the frost and crumbs from my lips and got ready to open the newspaper. Yet, what I saw on the front page was enough to send chills down my spine.

Girl with the spider tattoo murdered! Immediately, I began to read the article.

Another prostitute murdered. A young, brown skin female, in her late teens or early twenties, was found with her throat severed. The MO is proving to be the same psychological path of the killer suspected in the disappearances and deaths of now seven young women. Apparently, those young ladies were stalked or either sought out over the internet. An investigation is underway and because of the age being unclear and identity uncertain, there is no name to be released of the victim. Yet, this beautiful female had a very distinctive tattoo of a black widow spider over her left breast. If anyone knows anything or suspects that they know anything or suspects that they know who she is, please contact Crime Solvers at 555-432-1585.

At that instant, beads of sweat began to form on my brow. I mustered up enough strength to down the rest of the Latte and swallowed the last few bites of cheesecake. Instead of ordering anything else, I laid a two dollar tip on the table and left.

Right around the corner and just pass a Sbarro's Pizza spot was a few pay phones. I used the change I had gotten from the newspaper to place a call. I still hadn't had any access to my phone with the battery having gone dead. I couldn't pull up my phone contacts at all, so used to being able to retrieve a number from my call list. I couldn't seem to remember without it.

I toyed with the buttons on the pay phone for minute or so and dialed up the number I believed to be DaDa's. Nobody had answered her phone. I hung up before the answering machine could give its beep. Ironically, I hadn't got April's number through the course of events and she was the one that I needed to speak with the most. Instead, I dialed Labymba's cell number and she answered on the second ring.

"Good morning," I spoke into the receiver.

She responded with a soft voice, "Good morning to you Sir."

"There is a lot going on. Are you OK? Where are you?" I questioned.

"Yes," she answered. "I have just arrived in Miami and I am looking forward to being able to get back in town on Tuesday by 9:00 a.m. Please, understand that I won't miss our appointment for the world."

"I assume you can't talk and your date is accompanying you?"

"Yes," she said plainly.

"Did you see DaDa before you left?"

"Yes, I did."

"Was Fire with her?"

"Yes Sir."

"Make sure that you bring Daddy something home and Labymba please be safe honey."

"I will and thanks a bunch. You can expect me Tuesday."

"Goodbye."

That call was awkward. She couldn't talk and I hadn't said quite enough. Yet, I hoped that she gotten the hint. I left out of Union Station, exiting through the same doors I came in. I got into a yellow cab and the driver took "H" Street. We went up and over the bridge and road past the shops at 8th and "H" Street, a well-known spot for people to shop and get clothes, shoes, food, dope and coke.

We rode past Hechinger Mall and like always, there was a huge amount of people gathered together at the bus stop in front. The streets along that area were raggedy and we slowed and dipped in and out of a few potholes.

The cab zipped and made a left onto Minnesota Avenue. We rode past the Minnesota Avenue Metro Station and the driver made a right onto Sheriff Road and drove up to Eastern Avenue. We made a right on one of the avenues that a nigga had to be paying attention to at night. Up and down they would walk and always with something fitting and tight. If speeding, you might not be able to tell. A many have done been tricked because what they thought was a bad ass woman was a blister just dressed up real well.

At Foots Street, the driver made a right and a quick left onto 59th Street. The street was actually clear and I let the cab past my spot before I said anything. I wanted to survey the area thoroughly. It looked pretty cool, so I had him make a U-turn on the corner. While doing so, I spotted the rental car that April was driving on Eads Street. I paid the fare and got out.

When I walked into the apartment it didn't have any traces of being ransacked. If a police had been there, I damn sure couldn't tell. April was curled up on the couch under a large burgundy quilt. When I turned the corner to the living room, she looked up at me as

131

if she had seen a ghost. Her hair was pulled back into a ponytail and her eyes were puffy and red.

"Oh my God! I thought I lost you again."

April jumped up from the couch, exposing a white tank top, no bra, and a pair of black thongs. Vigorously, she jumped into my arms and wrapped her legs and feet around my waist.

"Damn! I thought I lost you Daddy."

"I'm good Ma, slow down." I said while squeezing her tight to let her know that my being there was definitely real.

After our heart-warming embrace, she helped me out of my jacket and shoes. Exhausted, I sat back on the couch and let the cushion conform to my tired ass body. April went into the bedroom and grabbed a backwood that one of the girls had prerolled of some Purple Haze. Then she went into the kitchen and grabbed two glasses and a half full bottle of Remy Martin VSOP. She poured us both a glass and snuggled up close to me then handed me the backwood and covered herself again with the quilt.

"What's going on April? Has anybody been here?"

"Well the landlord · · ·"

"Fuck the landlord! Has anyone been here?" I questioned.

"No! Only DaDa and Fire. They were here with me all night and the two of them left out this morning around 7:00 a.m. They were apparently up a little while before I had gotten up."

"Yeah! I can't wait to catch them two sneaky bitches," I said while firing up the backwood.

"The most important thing for you to know is, September was killed at that party Daddy. Labymba was in the room directly across the hall. I believe she knows something. Or the killer tried to get at her too. In the midst of all the confusion, she disappeared."

After exhaling a large cloud of smoke, I coughed a few times then cleared my throat and spoke, "Yeah!

I'm hip. The one thing about Labymba though is, if she knows it, she'll tell it to us. She may very well be a key to this twisted and bizarre ass puzzle."

"Where the hell is she?" asked April.

"I spoke with her this morning and she will be back early Tuesday morning and I'm wondering where the hell is Candy?"

I passed April the backwood and she refused. I took two good pulls and leaned up and sat it in the ash tray.

"Candy is alright Daddy. She left last night and said she was going to trap and trim some niggas. Candy walked up out of here saying hit her stupid ass on her twitter page. Nobody could convince that red bitch that you weren't alright."

"I like that," I said with a smile.

April looked up at me, "Well, now that you've found out how everybody is, ain't you concerned about me and how the hell I'm doing?"

"Of course I am. How are you Ms. April?" I asked with a grin.

She got up and removed the quilt off of herself. I watched her sexy self walk into the bedroom, with the thongs swallowed up in her ass. True enough, it had been a very long time since we had been intimate. April wanted me just as bad as I wanted her.

I quickly downed the rest of my drink. The backwood had gone out and I fired it back up, took a few pulls and just as I was staring down at the carpet, April screamed out, "Come here, wanna show you something!"

As I go up, I heard the sweet sounds of Prince playing from the bedroom stereo. Until the end of time, roared out loudly. With those smooth sound playing I didn't know what the hell I was in for. So, I quickly put the backwood out.

April had pulled all the blinds shut and lit one single candle on my night stand. You could see the glow from the fire dancing on the black, satin sheets. She lay on her side in the middle of the bed, naked, waiting.

For a minute, I just stood in the doorway. As I listened to Prince scream, I stared at her and realized that she was still so very beautiful. What I realized is that I still loved April and as she turned on her back, I realized how much I really wanted her.

I tore out of all my clothes and as I stepped towards the bed, her eyes took a glance at what she wanted so damn bad. My manhood became just as eager to see April. He swiftly rose to the occasion. There was no way that I could've just jumped on her though. I needed to taste her juices. I needed to explore who she was all over again.

At the bottom of the bed, I started and I first began by kissing on her red polished toes. April looked down at me and she smiled, and then closed her eyes. I lightly ran my tongue up her arch and she jumped and I moved on. I licked up the inner part of her thighs and she moaned and gripped the sheets with her matching red nails.

"Ooh! Take your time Spider."

"April had shaved and her pussy was so clean. I felt her body shiver when I licked over her mound. I weaved my body in between her legs and she opened them so that I could have my way with her.

I opened her pussy and stuck my tongue inside of her slowly. April scooted back and I chased her and stuck my tongue inside of her deeper. I heard her gasp and I went to her clit and began a slow rhythm of licks and in between a few passionate sucks.

"Yes! Eat this pussy Daddy." April stuttered.

I continued to tease her with my tongue while she squirmed and moved all about.

"Oh! Yes, right there. Oh yes!"

After long, April grabbed my head with both hands and began to fuck my face. Her juices were in my mustache and dripping from my beard.

"Lick it faster Daddy."

I speeded up my rhythm and took two fingers and inserted them inside of her slowly. This drove her crazy. So, at the same time, I fucked her with my fingers and licked on her clit with agile speed. April pressed down on my head so hard, I liked to suffocate. Then as I struggled to breathe and please her all at the same time, her body started convulsing.

She screamed out, "Oh shit! I'm cumming. Oh yes, yes Daddy, I'm coming!"

April jerked and I felt the spasms and the muscles in her pussy pulsate. I continued to lick until her movements slowed. Then instantly, it stopped and she lightly pushed me away so that she could recover.

"Damn! That was so good," said April in a voice that could barely be heard.

She lay there staring up at the ceiling and I smiled in the dim flickering light. April didn't need that long. She leaned over off the side of the bed and took a sip from her glass. I heard the ice tingling and assumed that I had given her just enough loving to make her sexy ass need a quench for her thirst.

On my back, I lay buck-a-naked while another one of Prince greatest hits played. As the candle burned down and the fire danced on the bedroom walls, Purple Rain churned out with melody.

"Oh shit!" I screamed out.

My back arched and I felt such a sensationable shock as the warm and cold feelings hit at the same time. April had put my dick into her mouth and her tongue ran underneath my shaft, while a piece of ice loosely bounced all around. It was an unexplainable pleasure and I laid back and enjoyed every single bit of it.

April deep throated the dick and the ice cubes ricocheted inside of her mouth, off her teeth and tongue. She sucked and then toyed with me so tantalizing at times.

"Damn! Work it girl!" I exclaimed.

She took my hard dick out of her mouth and by this time, the cube of ice had totally melted. The remainder of the chill could only be felt by the melted liquid, mixed with saliva, that ran down and around my balls. I lay in a small puddle while April continued to please me.

Her hand worked and jerked while she started sucking but without any ice in her mouth. This time she worked harder and much faster.

"Yeah! That's right," I said. "Eat this dick up."

I could feel the pressure rising and it was almost there. She was jerking and slurping and I arched my back and got ready to explode but April stopped just like that. I liked to had a heart attack. I was inches away. Yet, April rolled over on her back.

"I want you to make love to me and explode inside of me Daddy. I want you to love me right here, right now."

Before my erection could fade, I rolled over on top of her crazy ass and she opened her legs inviting me. As Prince screamed, I eased inside of her slowly and April clutched onto my shoulders with such a tight grip. Together we worked and our hips gyrated as if we trying to match one another moves. Together we sexed and shared passion. We shared a long lost pain and we began to sweat and continued to share an unbreakable love.

For what seemed like hours, we went at it. There was licking, biting on earlobes, necks and plenty of lust in the middle of it all. We fucked, we humped, we sweat and we made love. After several orgasms, the last one made us scream out together.

"I'm cumming!" I exclaimed.

"Oh shit! Me too Daddy. Damn! Yes, me too!"

It happened for us both at the very same time and it was so wonderful. We were both exhausted and had done our share of some powerful loving.

With barely any strength, I leaned over and grabbed the remote off the night stand and cut the stereo off. The candle had burned out completely. I laid on my back and April rest her head on my chest and pulled the cover up over us both. Then as we lay there in the dark, listening to each other breathe, the sounds of our hearts beating together, put us both to sleep.

Chapter 27

Somehow we both needed some rest. We had cuddled and kissed and even repositioned ourselves in the bed all day Sunday and slept all throughout Sunday night. I had gotten up early that Monday morning and went to the bathroom, wearing a pair of black silk boxers.

After I brushed my teeth and shaved, I decided to jump into the shower. I stepped out the bathroom and looked over at April in the bed and she was resting so peacefully. I left her alone and went into my walk in closet to pick me out an outfit for the day. It was dark and I stepped into the center and pulled on the chain and clicked on the light.

"What the hell?" I screamed out. "Somebody done been up in my shit!" I continued with rage.

April got up out of bed, completely naked and ran into the closet. She could clearly see the anger on my face. Yet, her own facial expression was blank. For a second, we both just stared there looking at one another dumbfounded.

"How in the hell could this happen, if you were here April?" I questioned while staring into her sleepy eyes.

"Wait a minute. This is a total shock to me Daddy. Somebody . . .

"Bitch!" I screamed. "Are you stupid?" You said those two funky ass bitches were here the other night and had gotten up early or some shit."

"Yeah! Only they would've needed a truck to carry all that shit up out of here," said April while looking around the closet again.

"Them bitches took all of my clothes, the working outfits and all of yall's shoes. Wow! Them bitches even took my shoes."

"There was a lot of money in this closet Daddy. The jewelry box is gone and so is that little safe you had back there."

"Get dressed April. Just let me try to and figure this shit out Ma. Find something for us both to wear."

I jumped in the shower first and as the steaming hot water ran over my body, I began thinking extremely hard. April had tried to warn me, yet I was convinced that I had all the answers. Unfortunately, my pimp hand was what was being questioned at that moment.

It had actually taken me several years to gain such a lavish shoe collection. I had animal and reptiles of all sorts that some men can't even phantom. Eel skin by Dan Post, mink, lizards, gators and crocodiles by Salvatore Ferragamo. I had rare soft shoes by Ermenegildo Zenga and Prada. Several loafers were among the exotic aggregation by Gucci, Mauri, Bally and some other Italian and English designers.

My most favorable was a pair of shoes that I never got the chance to wear. Labymba ordered them online and had them imported from Zimbabwe. They were a pair of Zebra hair, ankle high boots by Ceasar Paciotti.

The jewelry box had watches, chains and rings by several different jewelry makers. A lot of the items were collected by a many of the girls trapping and trimming. Exotic things they would clip from drunk tricks or those stupid enough to buy the ladies lavish gifts for sexual favors. Bvlgari, Cartier, Tiffany's and John Varvatos were among some of the diamond encrusted designer items that were now missing.

One side of that closet had belonged to the girls and they had their share of fine and rare things, which were now absent from the empty space. So many shoes, outfits and lingerie that would make men drool at the mouth. Catsuits, designer jackets, jeans and skirts of all sorts just to name a few. They had pocket books and handbags by Dooney & Burke, Gucci, Louis Vuitton, Marc Jacobs, Brunello Cucinelli, Yohji Yamamoto and Hermes. There was a lot of stuff in that closet space and although I was bothered about it being gone, I had been about to run away from it all. So, instead of dwelling on what was lost, I finished showering.

When I snatched the shower curtain back, April had found a pair of Nike boots that I had by the back door. She went into the hamper and retrieved a pair of old jeans and a black t-shirt and some clean shorts for me to throw on, out of one of my drawers. The clothes were on top of the toilet seat and the boots were on the floor by the stool. I got dressed and let her jump in the water behind me.

While April showered, I fired up a backwood and sat on the living room window sill. I was staring out into the street at four pigeons, pecking away at the core of what was once an apple. I inhaled deeply and pulled on the backwood nice and slow. Smoke escaped my nostrils a little and I blew out a heavy cloud. As the exotic relaxed me, suddenly it hit me.

I got up and went into the bedroom and got my phone off the charger. I hadn't used it in quite some time. I immediately dialed up DaDa's number and on the second ring I heard,

"The number you have reached is not in service."

I disconnected the call and scrolled through my phone book until I got to Candy and lightly tapped send.

"Hey Daddy!" she said when she answered.

"Where you at Sweet Thang?"

"I'm not too far from the house," she replied with intensity.

"Well, get here. I definitely need to see you."

"You'll be happy when you do; I'm sure as hell glad your cool. I'll be there shortly."

I hung up and after that call; I went online trying very desperately to access my account at the Bank of America. I followed all of the prompts and could have sworn that I tapped in all of the correct numbers to my account. I even entered my password of which the bank made all customers get to safeguard their transactions.

After the second try, I grew frustrated when I saw the screen display, *Please call you Bank of America.* It had been awhile since I had deposited any money into either of the accounts that I had with them, so I didn't panic. I figured that as soon as April got dressed, we could stop at the bank around the corner on Martin Luther King Highway.

Chapter 28

April got her clothes on and her dark skin was glowing. She brushed all of her hair back into a ponytail and it shined from the oil sheen she sprayed on it. April was wearing a tight pair of Dolce & Gabana jeans, some Nike Air Max and a black hoodie. Just as we were gathering our things and getting ready to leave a key turned in the door.

"I told you I was on my way. Where the hell yall headed?"

"The last time I checked, I was grown and the one laying the pimping down. Has the GAME changed?" I asked while looking Candy directly in her face.

She stepped into the living room wearing a skin tight one piece ensemble that revealed a vicious camel toe. Her braids were growing out from the roots and it was time for new do. Candy stared back at me in a sassy kind of way.

"No! The GAME ain't changed and your pimp hand is so strong, you need to look out the window and see just what your pimping do Daddy."

April looked at me with question, I looked at both of them, and then I walked over to the window and pulled the curtains back.

"Bitch! I know you ain't lost your damn mind and brought no nigga to where I lay my head."

April looked out the window over my shoulder, then asked,

"Who drives a red Caddy on chrome?"

Candy smiled, "The lame ass nigga who thought he was cracking slick, used to drive it."

"Bitch, state your case," I said coldly.

"Mr. Stay Down is what they call him. He slid up on me like he was trying to date. I figured that the nigga was trying to run GAME and I faked naïve and let the sucka play."

Candy fired up a cigarette in between talking and sat down on the arm of the couch. She kicked off her stilettos, revealing the black widow she had gotten tattooed on the top of her right foot. Her toenail polish was fuchsia and it was chipping and fading in several areas.

"Yeah!" said Candy. "A nigga know they gotta pay to play. So, he was willing to spend. I let him wine and dine me and I ate at the suckas expense. I ordered caviar, lobster and steak. I spent the GAME around and mashed on his ass so hard he couldn't get a break."

"Go ahead Bitch," said April as she listened with much approval.

"We ate, got naked and soaked in a Jacuzzi. He was trying with everything he had to wooh me. When that didn't work he put the dick on my some kind of good."

Candy took a long drag from her cigarette then continued, "I'm a bona fide whore and that may never change but the truth is, that nigga dicked me down. He didn't fuck me; he made love to me, like I was his woman. Then after it was over he started telling me how I would win if I got, with him. He bragged about his properties in California and Florida. Spoke about his bikes, cars and a banana boat. I'm already hip that pimping is dying down in the streets, and the crack heads and freaks are messing up the GAME. So, what he was talking about wasn't new to me."

"Like what?" I asked.

"Like some of what we do Daddy."

April handed Candy the ash tray and she twisted her cigarette butt out and then continued, "Dating through websites and utilizing the social media industry. How it can be deeper than just penetrating sex. Mr. Stay Down spoke about sexual fantasies and skits done with a web camera. About how far the business could be taken and how I could travel overseas without actually going. He was truly spitting good GAME to a bitch. Even tried to assure me how we would build a database with files to store our lavish clientele and the profiles of each existing member. Yeah! I faked like it was an awesome idea and I was still so undecided. So, look at what he did," Candy said, while dangling her hand in the air in front of herself.

"Oh shit!" April exclaimed.

I didn't reply I just stared at the diamond encrusted cluster he had given Candy. I wasn't impressed. Instead of talking about the cheap ass ring or even mentioning Stay Down's weak ass attempt at trying to knock my broad, I let her go on.

"Anyway," said Candy. "I gave him life and ate him up real good. Yes! Put his ass straight to sleep. After I was sure he was all the way out, I took everything, except his leopards."

"Leopard what?" I asked.

"Leather, leopard print, Speedo bikini drawers." Candy said with a smile. "That nigga was a super freak."

We all broke out into a laughter I looked over at April and she had tears in her eyes. Candy was smacking her leg and that had even tickled me.

Afterwards, April said, "Girl you a fool·"

"Shit ain't easy for us bitches trying to get a dollar· Then to top it all off, there is a fool out there trying to kill us to fuck· The GAME is crazy·"

"Yeah! That was some sad shit that happened to September·"

"April you're right," said Candy· "But I ain't got time to get emotional· I'm not sure which one of yall bitches is playing fare·"

With surprise and anger April responded, "What the hell you talking about Candy?"

"Yeah!" I added in· "Wuz up?"

"I got a text message from DaDa this morning· I'm gonna run out to the car and get my phone·"

"Hold up!" I stated· "Just what the hell it said·"

Candy fiddled her toes around, feeling for one of her stilettos without getting up off of the arm of the couch· She then slipped on the other heel and continued, "It was something about how nobody could play the GAME better than she could play· How she had enough money to feed for three without your selfish ass· Some other shit about how she kept telling you that she was supposed to be on your arm·"

"That bitch is crazy!" I screamed out·

"I believe she was pregnant Daddy," said Candy· "As a matter of fact, I'll be back· You need to read the damn messages for yourself·"

Candy got up and went to the front door· When she opened it, I heard the loud sounds of a helicopter over head· April looked at me with an unrecognizable stare, then she screamed out, "Hold up girl!"

She followed behind Candy and I shut the door behind the two· I needed a drink bad· Only me and April had downed the last of it· I went to the window after a minute or two, to see what was taking so damn long· When I sat up in the window sill and pulled the curtain back, I immediately spotted Candy and April in the front yard arguing.

They were gesticulating. Their necks were popping and heads twirling. I spent around and grabbed a piece of backwood out of the ash tray and fired it up. When I looked back out of the window, I saw April smack the shit out of Candy. Yet, she wasn't no scared ass chick. Candy fell back a few feet and kicked off her heels. The only thing April had time to do was accept her charge because Candy had rushed her with a fury of wild ass swings and some Mayweather type punches.

April held her ground and swung a good amount of blows her damn self. They were clutching and giving it to one another. It was more than evident that the two of them had some serious feelings they were trying to get off of their chest.

The GAME changed when Candy grabbed April's hair and smacked her repeatedly in the face. April couldn't take but so much. She stomped on Candy's left foot extremely hard, causing her to let go immediately. April hit her twice in the face then went low and gave a serious one to the gut. That shot bent Candy over in pain. Instead of April following up, she stepped back and whipped out a knife.

"Bitch! I'll kill you!" She screamed.

They were both breathing hard and damn near out of breath. Candy had some scratches on her face and April's clothes were torn a bit. A few knots were visible on the as well. Regardless, I wasn't gonna let them kill each other.

I cracked the window and yelled out, "Alright, that's enough! Yall stop all the carrying on in my yard!"

April looked up at the window real quick and rolled her eyes at me. She was brandishing a seven inch curved karambit blade. The sounds of the helicopter over head seemed to almost drown me out. Yet, I know she heard me. Candy didn't back down and it looked as if her body language was challenging April to bring it on. The sounds of sirens could be heard in the distance and they were screaming as the sounds seemed to be getting closer.

April eyed Candy up and down real good, while waving the Karambit in the air. The weapon is held by inserting the first finger into the hole at the top of the handle so that's its blade curves forward from the bottom of the fist. It's primarily used in a slashing or hooking kind of motion. The finger guard makes it difficult to disarm and allows the knife to be maneuvered in the fingers without losing one's grip.

"Bitch this ain't over," said April.

The sounds of the helicopter blades got louder and louder. April walked away reluctantly. She went up the hill towards Eads Street where she had parked the rental. I leaned in the window and notice Candy climbing into the Cadillac on the driver's side I lit up the remainder of the backwood that went out while the fight was going on.

Trash and debris seemed to be blowing about as if the wind was whirling about a storm. More than one siren screamed in the distance. Candy grabbed a laptop out of the trunk and had a purse on her arm. She shut the trunk and stepped out into the street, headed back to shut the driver's side door. When the all black, Dodge Charger hit the corner, it made the turn with such high velocity that two of its tires were off the ground. The driver tried to regain control of the vehicle and it fishtailed, and then quickly straightened back up.

The impact was devastating. Candy never saw it coming. She shut the Cadillac door and stepped into the street, only to be struck so hard that the Charger broke both of her legs on impact. Her body was thrown into the air, some thirty feet away. I was in awe as I watched Candy flip and her laptop went one way and money scattered throughout the air. She landed with a thud and her lifeless body lay leaned on the curb.

Blood ran slowly from her nose and mouth and her eyes were open, yet the chapter on her young life had been closed forever. Bills of all denominations, lay in the street and blew with the wind.

Behind the Dodge Charger not one, but three DC police patrol cars followed. All of them were so heavy on the chase that the lead the Charger had gained, caused them to miss Candy's body cracking the front windshield. Their suspect was in all attempts fleeing and with no intentions of being caught.

I damn near fainted. My mouth was wide open and I was in a state of total disbelief. I couldn't move and for however long it was, I sat in the window, until the backwood burned me and snapped me back to reality.

I was gonna run out of the front door but when I went to open the door, there was incredibly too much police activity. I ran to the back door in the kitchen and looked out into the alley. The entire neighborhood was surrounded. I had no way out. There were two unmarked cars double parked by some of the stolen vehicles and car parts.

I needed a drink. Unfortunately, the only thing left in the apartment was a bottle of yellow Nuvo that the girls had left in the refrigerator. I squat down on the kitchen floor and downed half of the bottle quickly. I couldn't believe what the hell was going on. It was too damn much. It was all ending and unlike anything I ever thought could happen to a Playa.

Sitting on the kitchen floor with the bottle in between my legs, it shocked me when my phone rang. I heard it and wasn't sure I was even hearing right. I reached into my pocket and it stopped ringing. Somebody had left me a text message.

Daddy, I've been in Miami now for long enough. I have seen that the world has so much to offer. I've visited such wonderful *places and been spoiled with luxurious shopping sprees. From France, Jamaica and this time at Bel Harbor Mall.*

A place where only the real wealthy frequent. Lamborghinis and Bentley Mulliner editions. I've even ate at restaurants I can not pronounce. Life is extremely good. Daddy you were the one to tell me to look for a man with sustenance and I believe that is exactly what I have found. Modern technology is so advanced that it may not seem fare to give it to you this way. Yet, I have chosen and I love you enough Daddy to serve you and I hope you will still respect the GAME. I no longer play for you and I will marry a man who owns a great deal in Miami. He is a man with stability. You are welcome to attend and I will inform you when we set a date. Thank you for really teaching me the GAME. Thank-you so much Daddy for showing me that the GAME does change.

Love always,
Labymba Junglist

When I saw the name, I couldn't believe that I had lost to a nigga who was sure enough official. A cat from Jamaica who owned several properties from New York on down the east coast. Chosen was just what Labymba did and I couldn't hate. Of course I had lost the baddest chick in my stable.

Suddenly my thoughts were interrupted with a loud banging on the door. I sat there on that kitchen floor, totally unable to move. I heard it when several feet ran up the back steps leading to the kitchen. Still I didn't move, I let the phone go and it fell on the ground next to me. I raised the bottle and there wasn't anything left to swallow. When they knocked the front door off the hinges, I wasn't surprised at all.

I looked up and several weapons were pointed down at me. The GAME was over, just like that.

With handcuffs squeezed incredibly tight on my wrist, I was escorted out the front door. There was an ambulance, a coroners van and fire trucks and police cars aligned on the street. People were all up and down 59th Street, North East.

Once I had been placed in back of the marked patrol car, I looked out of the window and saw several faces, Davin and Tanika Stewart; my neighbors were amongst the crowd. Ms. Pat and all her children, Tony and Jennel and even Big Tony. Carl Gee Perry was sitting on a milk crate smoking a black and mild. I spotted Joe Green and a few of his men. Richard and Cappricha were staring silently. Mark Mayo and Tina Mayo, Angie and her kids were watching from their front porches. Reggie Hicks, old fly ass was sipping on a bottle of Moet watching the spectacle unfold. Lil Greg (DC) Wellington Park finest gave me a strong head nod. I noticed Rick, Twin, Black-a-velli and two other good men blowing out a cloud of smoke off in the cut. John John and Peanut were walking up the sidewalk towards the patrol car. Latanya Clarke, Tracy Ford, Tanika Bailey, Vanessa Canady, Faline Chase, Gaye, Christina and Alanda Sharp were on the corner staring aimlessly. A few of those females were repping Breast Cancer Awareness to the fullest. I spotted more than one pair of pink Phoam Posits and pink 990 New Balance amongst the many. Then one in particular face shocked me. It was April among the many faces. She eyed me and I fought to read her lips, "I love you and I got you." The car pulled away from the curb.

Chapter 29

The officer who had been escorting me looked over his shoulder at me. I vaguely remember him being an older guy. Light skin, with a receding hair line, high cheek bones, grey in his mustache and beard.

"Son you've caused quite a stir and there is an officer outside of our district who seems to have a lot of interest in you Mr. Deters, you've become very popular," he said frankly.

"I ain't got no rap for you," I responded with disgust.

"Yeah! Maybe you don't but what you might need is to get your mind right young man. Adam Woods is willing to go through hell or high water to have you convicted."

"I ain't scared and I got a legal team that will shut shit all the way down."

The officer looked up in the rearview mirror at me, and then spoke with all seriousness. "Once the life of someone is lost, things are taken into a whole different context."

"I didn't kill anyone."

"I never mentioned that you did son. Your being charged with pandering, soliciting sex, trafficking sex, soliciting a minor, 1st degree assault, abduction and a few other charges."

"Damn!" I shouted.

"The only light you'll see is, if you give up a few major playas that are out there in the streets getting down."

"I ain't no fucking rat and I don't give a fuck about those damn charges."

"Then your best bet is to hope like hell that Adam Woods can get you a deal. Maybe they can drop some of your charges if you plead to the guns that we found in the wall of that apartment."

That is exactly what I felt like. Like a wall had actually came tumbling down on me and crushed me in the process of it all. I had played hard and I had thought that I would surely come out on top in the end.

The officer was still talking and I couldn't hear him at all. There was too much else racing through my mind. Somehow he eventually realized that I had no more to say. I stared out the window and then closed my eyes.

A few blocks from the White House, around the corner from the United States Capitol Building, drizzles of rain began lightly at first. The sounds of moving traffic could be heard on the wet pavement in the distance. As she walked across the parking lot, her thick ass hips bounced from side to side. Her movements were quick yet elegant. The rain had begun to stick to her pretty face. As her heels sloshed in and out of the puddles of water, she could've looked down at any time and seen her disshelved, brown skin, mirrored reflection bouncing back at herself.

She was tired, yet her brown eyes were open so wide and she was still rolling off the pills. She was frustrated, hurt and disgusted by the feeling of the warm semen that oozed from out of her and began to slowly trickle down her thigh.

With desperation, she weaved between several cars and trucks within the parking lot. As she searched for a certain vehicle, her Louis Vuitton satchel, bounced against one of her vivacious hip. It wasn't hardly enough to slow her down at all.

Then in an instant, her every move was cut completely short. She hadn't readied herself for death. She hadn't expected to meet her maker in the cold and in the rain. Nor did she dress for the occasion. It wasn't warm enough for a tight brown mini skirt, a low cut blouse, no stockings and a lot of cleavage.

With her hand on the hood of a Lincoln Navigator and one heel in the air, she made the attempt to turn by the truck. Yet four shots rang out simultaneously. She tumbled to the ground without a shoe on one foot and her short skirt rose just above her thighs. With barely any strength at all, she turned her head to look straight up into the direction of the moon. Then as she moaned and struggled to allow air to enter her mouth, nose and lungs. A face appeared. Directly in front of the white glow of the moon, was the face of her killer.

She could not see yet her vision was a total blur. She could see but she could not see clearly. A mouth was moving but her ears weren't working. She was confused, wounded and struggling for life. As she inhaled deeply and her sight faded in and out, she recognized it at once. What she saw was not a face; it was the barrel of my gun as it pointed directly down at her.

The first shot tore into her shoulder, rupturing her shoulder blades; the second shot missed and ricocheted off the pavement. The gun was warm and I fired two more shots into her mid-section and her body jumped with each thud. Life was escaping her and the rain began to fall harder. She laid in the parking lot bleeding, the rain and her blood both mixed together and swam frantically for the nearest drain.

Thunder crackled loud and roared with intensity. Flashes of lightening shattered the sky line in the distance, piercing the night sky. I bent over her and reached into her Louis Vuitton satchel and retrieved an iPad, hand held computer. Desperately I began to hit the power button. The screen displayed a large amount of money and I hit a few more keys and seen The Bank of America. Yet suddenly, water damage destroyed the picture.

"Hey!" said the officer.

I had awakened from a nap and could see the rain bouncing off of the front window. The streets were wet and the traffic was moving relatively slow. I didn't respond. I was still trying to register where we were at.

"If you want you can wave all the bullshit and I will take you straight to a cell. You're gonna have to go through interrogation at some point and time. I just assume that you're in need of some rest."

I reluctantly looked up into the rearview mirror and our eyes met. He was more than right. Running for your damn life ain't an easy job at all. I didn't want to be placed in a cell. The sheets weren't gonna be satin. I was accustomed to such a lavish life that seemed to be ending right before my eyes.

"Officer, please by past all that and let me get a cell and a phone call. I would appreciate that more than anything." I said.

"Son, I am gonna grant you that one wish because I know that you need it."

"Thanks," I responded.

I looked out of the side window and lightening flashed in the sky line. As the thunder roared, I looked into a dark colored sedan and could have sworn I saw April behind the wheel of the vehicle. Quickly I shook my head and tried to erase that out of my thoughts.

April deserved ten times more but I wasn't able to nurture her. I had been selfish to even ask her to teach me how to love her. My mind was concentrating on money and getting away. For the likes of me I was unsuccessful in both attempts.

The handcuffs felt like they were cutting off y circulation, so I shifted and moved my hands to the opposite side. Then suddenly, I felt a swerve, and then I heard, "Boom! Clash! Booommm!"

The car spun around in circles and I couldn't quite register anything. Then I heard, "Crash! Splish! Boom!"

My head bounced off of something and as the blood ran down my face, I couldn't tell if it had come from the shattered window or another object in the vehicle. I was lying sideways when the car had stopped spinning. My shoulder was in so much pain that I had tears in my eyes. My body was crammed in between what felt like a large piece of metal.

For a while I lay there and although I couldn't move, I could still hear the traffic on the pavement in the distance. Then I saw him move slowly.

"10, 29, somebody come in."

A set of boots that belonged to a female sloshed up next to where we sat and I went out.

I vaguely remember the explosion but could definitely taste the blood as it trickled down from my head, ran along the side of my face and into my mouth. The rain fell down upon me as my body was being dragged back towards a dark colored sedan.

The fuel from the police cruiser had spilled out onto the wet pavement. Oddly enough, the light rain couldn't stop such a devastating blast of metal. Pieces scattered, several windows burst as flames ignited into the misty air. Rubber burned, smoke became heavy and ironically another crash, split, boom sounded as more cars joined the pile up. Sirens screamed louder and louder from what sounded like all emergency response units, rushing to the area in the on-going lane of I-295.

I was put in the back of the unknown vehicle and laid across the back seat. Whether to conceal my identity or keep my body from shivering a perfume smelling, navy blue colored blanket was thrown over me entirely. I inhaled the sweet aroma and licked over my lips to taste the blood again. Then I passed out as my body heat began to warm me under the blanket.

At some point and time later, I awoke to hear the car radio playing through the back speakers. There was a broadcast from the radio news, giving details of a severe thunderstorm blowing through the DC, Maryland and Virginia areas. Heavy rain beat against the windows and the windshield wipers moved rapidly.

As the car traveled, I could feel the bumps. My right side ached terribly and there was a sharp pain that I couldn't discern as I only felt it whenever I inhaled deeply. I wiggled my toes, and then I tried to move my fingers. My body shifted as we took a corner with speed. Then another jolt and more speed.

Once again I faded out of consciousness.

"CoCo I haven't been to see you in a while and right now, I need you," said April.

"Yeah! That is obviously clear. Ain't nothing changed BITCH! I'm still same. I told you when we were in Danbury, Connecticut that you could always count on me. Especially after you cut Faline across the face with that razor and ripped her hair out. That pretty yellow BITCH tried to get at me that morning and if it wasn't for you April, I might have really been fucked up real bad."

"I don't have much at all," said CoCo with all seriousness. "Yet what I do have, I'm always willing to share it with a go hard BITCH that I fucks with."

April smiled at her old friend, "I'm gonna need some first aid supplies. A few things to clean up my man."

"I'll get you some wash cloths, towels, some alcohol and a few clean t-shirts for the both of you to throw on. Yall can go ahead and get cleaned up and get some damn rest."

"Thanks! We're gonna need it."

"April, I played that GAME and when I played, I broke every single rule. I played so damn hard that I've been fouled out with no chances of returning. I'm sick now and all I wanna do is leave some kind of good legacy behind with my kids and every other person that I fuck with."

April didn't speak she just stared at CoCo dumbfounded. True enough, CoCo and April were in the Feds together and they had both gone through some things in the joint. None of that mattered. CoCo stood on loyalty and respect and vowed to always show that to a friend especially one in need.

CoCo was real dark skin and with huge, coal black eyes. Her lips were big and April teased her about how juicy her bottom lip always looked. She had a little acne on her face but nothing grotesque. She wasn't ugly but she wasn't all that cute either.

CoCo was tall and fairly thin. Her hair was short and she wore it all going back in eight cornrowed braids. Her labra were pierced. She often clicked a red ball off her teeth or toyed around with it in her mouth, displaying an eager tongue at times. She was known as Jasper in the streets.

"Look! My house is big enough for you to lay your head for a while April. Ain't nobody here but me, my niece Ximora, Kasha and my son Darin. You two can get right. I ain't got a lot of food but I got space. Yall are gonna have to make do on the couch."

"That's cool," said April as she looked over at the raggedy tattered and torn piece of furniture.

CoCo had helped April carry me from the car and into the house. Hours had passed and I still slept in a coma like sleep.

The couch was a floral print, both orange and tan, yet it was stained in multiple areas. The cushions were torn and the stitching was damaged. The springs underneath me were poking through parts of the fabric. I couldn't feel it then and my body had sunk deep into a form of relaxation as the raggedy ass couch seemed to form around my sore and wounded limbs.

Once again, I was running for my life. Another journey towards freedom that I was hoping would eventually come. I had been unknowingly helped out of one mean ass uncompromising position. Yet I was thrown into another hap-hazard that I hadn't anticipated at all. Desperately I was switching lanes through life trying to get it right.

While still suffering from so much pain, I awoke at 2:04 a.m. that same night. I looked up and April was staring down into my eyes. She had her feet on both sides of my head pointing in the direction of my own. She sat directly over top of e on the arm of the couch. April seemed to be twisting or fiddling with her hair.

"Hey Daddy! You alright?"

I tried to move but too much of that, wasn't happening. Pain seemed to surge through several parts of my body. I moaned at the uncomfortableness then figured it best to remain still. Lying on my back, I stared up at April.

"I'm sore as hell but I'm cool," I said in a very low tone, next to a whisper.

"Your alive Daddy and above anything else, you ain't in jail."

That is definitely true. You've made the impossible happen Bitch. I respect all the work you put in. But tell me where the hell we're at?" I asked.

"We're in Northeast on 15ᵗʰ Street Daddy!"

"What?" I questioned. "What the hell are we doing around Montana? Why the hell didn't you take me up and out of DC?"

"I drove around for hours Spider. Give me a break. I had to get somewhere where I could trust someone and we could get some rest and eat."

"Yeah! Well I guess this will have to do then. I do know one young nigga from around here who I could get at. Matter of fact, Seven could probably help us out."

At that moment I heard a rattling noise coming from the kitchen. I looked at April strangely and her eyes were as wide as mine. I used a finger over my mouth to say hush. We stared at one another and listened. Then abruptly April spoke.

"It's the rats. Spider it's the rats Daddy. Their running from eye to eye on the stove."

"What?"

"Yeah! They're feeding off of the scraps left on the stove from cooking. Either that or they're "just scurrying around for water. A lot of times they will eat the pieces of meat and crumbs trapped in the grease."

"Damn!" I said with astonishment.

"Turn your head and look over there by the door. This place is infested. Look how big they are."

Sure enough, there was an old radiator heater by the door. More than a dozen large rats were sniffing and rummaging in that area. My eyes followed what looked like two other rodents that shot across the carpet fast. Both of them were heading to hide under the same couch we were on.

Boss Playa or not, I had never had any love for the creatures. Dirty ass rodents with no backbones. They were capable of reproducing in large numbers and had no problems running people up and out of their homes.

Rodent or human, I despised the other one as well. Rats, the contemptible person who was more heartless than anything and who'd betray his friends or associates for any reason at all.

Although I was hurting, I slightly cringed. April noticed my subtle movements and could obviously tell that I was indeed bothered by their heavy presence. The rats weren't playing and their red eyes glowed in the darkness.

"Daddy get you some rest. I'll watch over you while you sleep. Go ahead and rest."

"Before I do that, tell me who's house this is April?" I questioned with sincerity.

"It belongs to an old hard leg. She been out the GAME for a long time now. She squared up some years back and got caught up in some type of Circus Love."

"What you mean?" I asked.

"The old dude that she booed up with used to be one of her biggest tricks. They both contracted the HIV virus. Ain't no telling who the hell gave it to who? I ain't gonna speak bad about the bitch. They made it do what it do and she got two healthy kids out of the deal."

"Sooner or later everybody squares up. Either that or they die playing as hard as they can play April."

"So what you thinking about four corners Spider? You trying to convince me that this is it for a no good ass pimp like you?"

"I never said that," I shot back with a coy look in my eyes.

"You don't need to say one more word. Whether you're pimping or playing or just an ordinary Playa, I'm the one bitch who's got your back, your sides and you front. Recognize Daddy, that I'm gonna be with you until the wheels fall off."

Chapter 30

Fire held DaDa's hand as they both walked away from the touch screen kiosk. It had taken them a while to figure out how to work the computerized machine at the Washington Reagan National Airport. Ironically, it sat right beside the desk and one of the ticket agents was nice enough to give the ladies some instructions.

"Good thing that African lady got us through that one. I was seriously getting frustrated."

"Calm down Fire. We gotta get on the plane now and we good," said DaDa.

With a huge smile and a bright look in her green eyes, Fire shot back, "You gonna lick my pussy while we lay on the white sandy beach?"

"I'm gonna do more than that to your sexy freckled face ass. I'm gonna buy you a big house in Brazil and stare at you while you prance around in some thongs."

"Yeah! Don't get it twisted and think that I'm gonna get turned out and let you and anybody else be playing all in my butt."

"Wow!"

"Yeah! They say that's all their into over there. I don't know why you picked Brazil. They even have a real high AIDS rate."

DaDa looked up into Fire's eyes, without blinking, *"So does DC so what's the damn difference? With gay marriages being legal everywhere there is no wonder about the high rate of AIDS or the open practice of homosexuality.*

You're all the way in the GAME now Fire, so you can't twist your face. Even if it is your first time."

Fire didn't speak, she just rolled her eyes. They were headed towards an area within the airport with a few restaurants. For some reason everyone seemed to be moving so fast. Quickly, they walked past a Dunkin Doughnuts and the rich and strong aroma of cheap coffee filled the air. DaDa and Fire both glanced over at the glazed and iced cakes and doughnuts in the glass display case. Even if they wanted to stop, the wait for anything would be extremely long. The line was stretched out with eager coffee sippers and those wanting Frappuccino's and pastries.

They passed by a large wall covered mirror. Their reflections stared back at them. With a side glance, Fire's hips poked out and her plump ass protruded in a real tight pair of black, BCBG stretch jeans. Her feet were in a jazzy pair of black sandals. The red polish on her toes matched the red thin blouse that she wore. Draped over her shoulder was large, red leather, duffle bag by Coach.

DaDa walked behind Fire slightly so an image of her own self was visible in the mirror as well. Her brown Gucci heels matched her brown mini skirt. DaDa had on a low cut blouse that accented her breast. Yet the cream color and thin fabric would hold onto a stain with no problem.

Up ahead was a small eatery with several restaurants. There was a Wendy's, Sbarro's Pizza,

Steak-n-Shake, Taco Bell, Wong Chow and a few other fast food spots· Just as they were nearing the corner to them all DaDa's iPhone rang·

"Hello," she answered while in mid stride·

Fire looked back noticing and then the both of them stopped so that Da Da could handle the call· Fire stared down at her with an inquisitive look·

"Hey there!" Came the male voice on the other side of the line·

"I need to see you one last time·"

"You can't," said DaDa·

"Give me a good damn reason why I can't·"

"I'm waiting for my flight·"

"That ain't good enough· I wanna taste you one more time on my lips·"

"Sorry," said DaDa·

"You're saying sorry but that isn't good enough· I want you to meet me at the entrance where I dropped you two off at in about five minutes·"

"For what?" she asked·

"I've got you pretty ass Louis Vuitton satchel and a couple hundred more dollars for you if that's what the hell it'll take·"

"Don't do that to me· You already know it's not about money with us any longer· Your making this oh so complicated for me· I mean damn· We're already dressed for the trip and everything·"

"And?"

"And it's crazy you've got my stuff· Damn! I need that·" DaDa said with disgust·

"I need your body· To be honest I don't want you to leave· I feel as if I've invested so much in our relationship· Letting you fly away from me to another side of the world is painful·"

"Look! Stop talking crazy· We will be there· Have the heat on and don't you expect a long ass visit· We've got a flight that leaves at 1:55 a·m· so that gives you close to an hour, to say what you gotta say and return what you got."

"I'll be there Sweetie."

With disgust, DaDa disconnected the line and turned towards Fire. They were standing not too far from the entrance to the eatery.

"What?" asked Fire? "Who in the hell was that?"

"The question is why the hell didn't you pay closer attention when you were packing our things?"

With a puzzled look, Fire shot back, "I don't know what you're talking about. I've got everything in my duffle."

"You were so busy concentrating on smoking that last backwood that you forgot my fucking Louis bag."

"Oh shit." Exclaimed Fire.

"We're talking about close to a $100,000 and I need that damn computer to access not only the account of the money we took from Spider but also to access the Brazilian account that I had the other $420,000 put in."

"Damn! I'm sorry."

"Fuck being sorry. You gotta pay much more attention to what you doing. Unless you want me to leave your ass in Southeast. There damn sure is enough bullshit running around Ward 7 for you to get into something a lot less lavish."

"No! I'm sorry again baby. I fucked up but I'm with you. I'm following your lead."

Instead of eating, they turned completely around and headed for the escalator. Once they took the ride down to the next floor, they got off and began to walk with speed. Overhead were signs displaying a many of the different airline services. United Airways, American Airlines, TWA, Jet Blue, British Airways and several others. Unlike the many patrons who were rushing to board flights, they were headed the complete opposite way.

When the ladies arrived at the entrance and exit area, the chill of air could be felt. The automatic doors were funneling people in and out that were destined to arrive or leave for their departure from the Metropolitan area during the morning hours.

"That's his car over there," said DaDa while pointing. "This trick was obviously already here. Or probably never even left."

"The power of the pussy is ultimately incredible baby." Fire said with a smile.

"You ain't never lied about that."

"We got enough time to make this fool buy us something to eat. That's the least thing he could do."

"Fire don't you go trying to wooh this nigga. Matter of fact, just lay back Baby and let me work. Here, pop this Superman and chill, said DaDa with a small red pill extended towards her lover. After it was grabbed, DaDa took one herself. Just a little geeked up the ladies used a few heavy swallows to force the pills down.

Together they approached a black Lincoln Continental and a light drizzle of rain fell down over their shoulders. The fumes from the exhaust spewed out into the chill night air as they stepped up to the car from the rear. Fire got in the back seat and DaDa picked the Louis Vuitton bag off the front seat and put it on her lap. After both doors were shut, the car pulled away from the curb quickly.

True enough, the velour seat made Fire relax and get herself comfortable. She could hear the wildest music coming from the back speakers as it played in a mid-high tone. Fire wasn't hip to Mozart and the distinct sounds of the piano were intriguing to her virgin ears.

Fire examined the back area of the car and it was miraculously clean. The only thing she noticed was a bag on the floor with the initials A.W. stitched into the brown leather material. She didn't bother it but instead tried to peer out of the limo tinted windows and into the street.

After minutes of riding, Fire glanced up into the rearview mirror and some coal black, slanted eyes were staring back at her. Outside of his thick eyebrows and the bridge of his nose, she couldn't recognize him. His stare was so piercing that it forced her to look away.

"Where the hell do you think you're taking us?" Asked DaDa.

A clicking sound from the power locks could be heard. Yet he didn't respond to her comment.

"Look! We have a flight in close to an hour," she continued. "You're already headed back over the 14th Street Bridge. Make a stop so that we can eat and talk, please."

"I'm not interested in a whole lot of talking." He said finally.

"I know your sour but I've got to go. You're aware of how much shit I've caused. Besides, whenever you take your vacation time you can come and spend time with me and the baby."

"That's the one part that drives me crazy. I've fallen so in love with you that I'm willing to take care of another man's baby."

"You don't have to! I can make it on my fucking own! Me and my child."

"Face it! I've fallen so over heels for you that I've been willing to compromise my own damn life."

"And?"

"And, I won't let you be alone. Or with anyone else for that matter I refuse to let your sexy little ass go."

"You're sick!"

"Just maybe I am," he said then began to laugh such an irritable laugh.

DaDa stared out of the window at the city lights, and then suddenly she questioned him, "Why are you driving so fast?"

With both of his hands inside of black leather gloves, he held onto the steering wheel with a firm grip· The speedometer read 74 mph and it was slowly increasing· Yet his foot didn't lighten up on the gas pedal·

"Slow down!" DaDa hollered·

He quickly looked over at her then back towards the road again· "That's what I did," he said· "I slowed down long enough to get caught up playing this vicious game with you but I have to be the winner in the end·"

DaDa saw a sign that read, *South Capitol Street ½ mile*· They were headed up I-295 and the elevation of speed had obviously caught Fire's attention· With grave interest, she leaned up in between the two seats·

"Hey!"

Unfortunately, that was her last word she ever spoke· While DaDa turned in her seat to respond, he quickly retrieved a black, Glock 17, 9 mm, semi-automatic handgun from the right side of his shoulder holster· The gun had been concealed by his jacket·

He wasted no time at all· His actions were so quick that DaDa never got a chance to say anything· With the same left hand, he turned his upper body slightly and shot fire in her forehead one time· The blast was so devastating that it made DaDa's ears ring· After the shot was fired DaDa spun around in her seat real fast and immediately stared back out of the front windshield· Shock and pure terror was written all over her face·

Fire's brain had exploded out of her skull and all over the backseat of the vehicle· Her lifeless body slumped down in an awkward position behind the driver's seat· Ironically, Fire died with her eyes wide open and her lips slightly parted· The distinctive small gap in between her two front teeth was visible· The puzzled look on her face clearly showed that she wasn't at all ready to leave this world.

DaDa had lost her partner within an instant and the one friend who could truly understand who she was. Every kiss between the two was passionate. They would laugh, smile and playfully suck on each other's lips. They were both still so very young so it wasn't hard for them to get along. Their hardest accomplishment was keeping their feelings away from me and the rest of the girls.

What started out as a ménages a trios' became so much more over time. I hadn't noticed and right under my nose these two young ladies had fallen in love. So in love that they attempted to deceive me and run away with every pimping dollar I had.

Love between them was so powerful that when April came back into the picture neither of them put up a fuss. Instead of cat fighting and competing for my attention, these two were paying attention to one another. I had been foolish and even sent them out together on shopping sprees. DaDa had picked out a lot of Fire's lingerie and got her to model it before she went out on dates.

Late nights together, not only getting money but getting it on. They were young inexperienced lovers whom learned how to spoil one another's bodies. They laughed and showered together, sometimes playing in the bathroom for hours whenever I wasn't at the apartment.

DaDa had poured her soul out and divulged parts of her past to her young lover. She had cried and explained to Fire how she had received the three cigarette burns on her left butt cheek. She not only told Fire about her being raped several times but that she felt like it was her own fault that it happened. DaDa had an ugly scar under her right nipple form one of her many fights with her stepfather. He had bitten her during one of his drunk fits of rage and forced

DaDa down on the floor in the kitchen. Her mother was asleep down the hall and when he bit her she had wanted to scream out in pain. The exact same way she wanted so badly to scream out after seeing Fire shot at point blank range.

DaDa suddenly realized that the driver was pointing the barrel of the weapon directly at her.

"Your best bet is to continue to be quiet. I told you that I didn't want you to leave me. Did you think for one damn minute that I would let you fly off into another country with her?"

Tears began to spill out of DaDa's eyes but still she didn't say one single word. Suddenly her body shifted as the car made an illegal U-turn at the firs light off the ramp.

"What the hell are you doing? She asked finally.

"I'm wondering if I should kill you or not you little sheisty bitch!"

"Fuck you!" DaDa screamed as more and more tears began to stream down her face.

Without being able to control it any longer, she began to sob. She bent down and put her face in her hands and began to let go. DaDa not only cried for the death of her lover fire but she cried many tears for all of her own emotional pain and strife. She grieved for a life full of hurt and misguided attention. DaDa cried for the confusion of her not knowing which way to go in life. She cried because she had become a prostitute and wound up in one hell of a life threatening situation.

DaDa head was down long enough for her not to notice exactly which way the driver had taken her. What she did notice was that they were in a large parking lot and the US Capitol Building seemed to look so very close.

When the driver's door opened, the heavy rain could be heard, along with the chimes from the door being ajar. DaDa was shocked when her door was opened a few seconds later. Instead of snatching her out into

169

the rain, the large man pushed her over forcefully and got in on her side of the vehicle.

DaDa scrambled for the door handle on the driver's side. A violent blow to her head kept her from reaching it. She tried hard to fight her assailant. He was too strong and too powerful for her. After flailing her arms and legs, he began to beat her in her face repeatedly. Blood ran from her pudgy little nose down into her mouth. One of her eyes was swollen and although she gave up fighting him, she could see him hovering over top of her. He began fiddling with his zipper.

"You're gonna give me some of that young pussy. I'm gonna fuck you this time and you're gonna be the one that pays for it."

DaDa closed her eyes and grimaced as he entered her frail body and began to rape her. She could smell alcohol on his breath and the heavy breathing on her neck sent chills down her spine.

He pounced up and down on her and kept her arms pinned above her head. At times he would stop and just look at down on DaDa with malice in his eyes. Sweat dripped down and mixed with some of the still warm blood that oozed out from her wounds.

Rushing to release his orgasm, he began to pounce on her much faster. He let her arms go and his own hands began to move around. Just as he had been about to climax, he reached his left hand behind the center armrest and felt around. With more speed he pounced on DaDa and finally reached his goal. While releasing all of his fluids inside of her he smeared Fire's blood all over her face. Then afterwards he fell upon her and whispered in DaDa's ear, "Damn I love you."

Chapter 31

    A many of women have endured unwanted sexual encounters. Lying underneath a man while they patiently waited for him to finish enjoying himself only. Sex she didn't enjoy nor want yet she closed her eyes, bared through the event for so many countless amount of reasons. For DaDa this wasn't an uncommon thing. She had been taught how to have sex without feelings. On several occasions, she coached the other females not to become intimate with any of the clients. She advised the not to engage in kissing or anything else that would make them feel passionate with the men who paid for their services.

    DaDa felt relieved when he finally removed his heavy frame up and off of her. Sweat covered her blouse and dried blood was on both the blouse and her pretty face. Yet she blinked several times to adjust her vision, noticing that he was out of the vehicle.

    After adjusting his zipper and belt, he looked over at her and smiled then spoke reassuringly. "You look a mess Baby. That was some incredible loving. But I can't leave you looking like that. I've gotta get some towels and things out of the trunk so that we can clean up a little. I'm gonna take you somewhere nice. That's the least thing I could do since you're staying with me," he said then laughed a loud, shrill and very irritable laugh.

When the driver's door opened, the chime sounded again. The sound of the rain beating against the asphalt could be heard and then the door slammed and there was complete silence. DaDa knew that this was her one moment. This was her time if any to change the course of the entire situation. It was dark and the front windshield was covered with droplets of water.

DaDa began to sob. She turned around in her seat and looked in the back at Fire.

"Damn Baby," she said in between tears. "I've gotta leave you. I love you with every inch of who I am. Please believe that I never meant for things to turn out like this."

DaDa grabbed her bag off the floor. After she looked into the side mirror and couldn't see him, she slowly opened the car door. Thunder crackled loudly, obscuring the sounds of the door chimes. She crouched down in the rain. DaDa had no idea where she was. All she knew is that this was not a dream and she was attempting to run for her life. So with desperation she weaved between several cars and trucks within the parking lot.

As she searched for any unlocked vehicle, her Louis Vuitton satchel, bounced against one of her vivacious hips. It wasn't hardly enough to slow her down at all. Then in an instant her every move was cut completely short. She hadn't readied herself for death. She hadn't expected to meet her maker in the cold and in the rain. Nor did she dress for the occasion. It wasn't warm enough for a tight brown mini skirt, a low cut blouse, no stockings and a lot of cleavage.

With her hand on the hood of a Lincoln Navigator and one heel in the air, she made the attempt to turn by the truck. Yet four shots rang out simultaneously. She tumbled to the ground without a shoe on one foot and her short skirt rose just above her thighs. With barely any strength at all she turned her head to look straight up into the direction of the moon. Then as she moaned and struggled to allow air to enter her mouth, nose and lungs, a face appeared. Directly in front of the white glow of the moon, was the face of her killer.

She could see yet her vision was a total blur. She could see but she could not see clearly. A mouth was moving but her ears weren't working. She was confused, wounded and struggling for life. As she inhaled deeply and her sight faded in and out, she recognized it at once. What she saw was not a face it was the barrel of the gun as it pointed directly down at her.

"I told you that I would never let you leave me. But since you're so persistent. I'm gonna give you a way out." He said with anger.

"Blam!!!" The first shot tore into her shoulder, rupturing her shoulder blade. DaDa screamed out in agony.

"Blam!!!" The second shot missed and ricocheted off the pavement.

The shooter fired two more shots into her mid-section "Blam!!! Blam!!!" and her body jumped with each thud. Life was escaping her and the rain began to fall harder. She laid in the parking lot bleeding, the rain and her blood both mixed together and swam frantically for the nearest drain.

Thunder crackled loud and roared with intensity. Flashes of lightening shattered the sky line in the distance, piercing the night sky. Her killer bent over her and grabbed her Louis Vuitton satchel. Sirens screamed out in the distance and more thunder roared in the sky.

Akil Dorsey Sr.

The killer jogged back towards his vehicle. As he approached the car, he slowed then looked around to see if anyone had been watching. Then after he got in the car, he closed the door and drove away slowly.

Chapter 32

"Spider! Spider! It's OK Daddy," said April as she wiped sweat off my forehead.

"Damn!" I responded then looked around frantically. "We're supposed to be in the Marriot."

"Nah Daddy, you're dreaming a little too damn much. We're still at CoCo's and tomorrow we can make a few phone calls and set up some plans so that we can get up out of here."

"What time is it?" I asked after cleaning the corner of my eyes.

"It's almost 5:00 a.m. Somebody knocked on the back door while you were asleep. CoCo answered from upstairs, out of her back window. She came down and asked if we were cool and she slid out the back door telling me to lock it behind her."

"Is she back yet?"

"No, not yet."

"Help me up," I demanded.

April didn't argue. She did just as I had asked. I went from laying on my back to sitting in the up right position with my back leaned up against the arm of the sofa. April sat down on the middle cushion.

"Your hair looks cute. Wow! You did all that while I was asleep?" I asked.

"Yeah Daddy. I wanted you to get your rest. Those rats were running rampant through this old ass house."

"I don't see any now."

"That's because the sun is about to come up. They enjoy the night life just like us."

"Knock! Knock! Knock!"

"That must be CoCo," I assured her.

"I got it," she responded.

"Make sure you look out the window April. Pay attention Bitch! Pay attention."

April walked across the stained carpet in her socks and the old floor squeaked in different areas. Just as we had both assumed they were all gone, a large rat shot across the dining room floor with what looked like a corn chip in its mouth. The rodent disappeared in a crack at the baseboard, underneath the window.

"Damn!" I cursed when I saw the tail slither in the hole behind the creature.

Minutes later, April emerged with CoCo. Only they had a guest of whom I clearly wasn't expecting at all.

Across from the old tattered couch, sat a love seat and two metal, folding style chairs. After the back door was locked and secured, everyone came in the living room and found themselves a seat. The ladies sat down on the metal chairs and their guest threw two large, black duffle bags down on the love seat and sat down himself.

CoCo looked up at me with her eyes as wide as fifty cents pieces. April fell back and played her position. After talking the hood off of a large black hoodie, the guest shook his golden brown dreadlocks free. He took a small, clear zip lock bag out of his pocket and handed the bag and its contents to CoCo. She put it in her bra and then winked at her guest.

It was at that moment, that I recognized this light skinned dude. His freckles and the few moles on his face were definitely distinctive.

"Just tell me that you ain't up in this trap spot getting high."

"Hell nah!" I said in disbelief. "What's good Seven?"

"Ain't shit! It's been a long time Spider."

"I'll agree to that." I stated frankly.

"Well, as you can see by these army fatigues that I'm wearing. I'm still out here trying to make it do what it do. Every single day above ground, I'm hustling to provide for me and my family. The question is what the hell got you around here?"

"I crashed, flat out."

"What you mean, you crashed?"

"Let's just say that I got into one hell of an accident trying to get away from them people."

"Wow! Pimp down. This looks like a muthafucking pimp in distress."

Everybody began laughing. CoCo saw it as her moment to get away. She eased off and went upstairs.

"On a serious note, pimping ain't too sweet in the street right now. Remember that fool they call Pimp Stay Down."

"Yeah! What about him?" I asked.

"He got caught up in a real bad situation. Some young nigga named Black Mike with a missing tooth from uptown, got at him."

"What?" questioned April as she joined in on our conversation. "You mean the Black that used to be with No Limit?"

"Yeah! That's him." Said Seven.

"What happened?" she asked.

Seven lit up a backwood and blew out the first cloud of smoke then he answered her. "Shit got real ugly for a pimp. Apparently Stay Down turned out Black's little sister."

"Agee. Damn! She was a beautiful young chick that was headed great places."

"Yeah that's her name Agee," said Seven. "Anyway they told him he could pay his way up out the situation. Only Stay Down bullshitted with that bread. So you know what the lick read."

"Yeah," I said. "Them niggas went and got what was theirs."

"Flat out," said Seven while passing me he backwod. He continued "The sad part is they made off with half a million that they got out of one of his houses in Florida. The money was under the stove top."

"What you mean under the stovetop?" asked April.

"Stay Down hid it in a good spot," said Seven. "The fire didn't touch one single bill of the money. The goons wound up burning him and thee of his hoes all face down in his basement. Each one was shot once in the back of the head."

"Damn! Sound like pimping got real sour for a Playa. Now that's what I call a pimp down."

"Yeah Daddy," said April. "A pimp who lost and ain't got no chances left I the GAME."

I smiled over at her then reached out to pass her the backwood that we had all been smoking on. I believe that April or anyone of the other girls would've died before they let somebody else get my money. But how was I supposed to know when I had been played out of pocket myself.

"Look here Spider. I came up on a lick tonight. I got a few things up in these bags that might put a smile on your face."

April go up and went into the kitchen to discard the rest of the backwood. When she walked back into the living room, her eyes grew just as wide as mine.

Seven bean to take things out the bag and lay them on the love seat. April sat back down in the metal chair.

"Shit looks crazy right?" Asked Seven as he stood over the items.

"Yeah!" I said. "You came off like shit."

"Me and a few of my men caught a fool slipping at the car wash. He was suspect for a straight up robbery but we came up. We got two bullet proof vest, a M1 assault rifle, two 9 mm's, some hitting ass, police style, cargo pants and a Louis Vuitton bag with a few boxes of bullets."

"Sound like you done got a pig."

"It don't make a difference," said Seven. "This fool was inside the car going through the cycle."

"And?"

"And we followed him. The wildest part is that after we caught him sliding up in the car wash all late in the night, he was on some straight bullshit."

"What the hell was he doing?" I asked.

"He was in the back of the car rubbing on the seats masturbating."

"Damn!" said April. "What kind of sick fool."

"Hold up!" I said while cutting her off. "How the hell did the rest of that play out?"

Seven pointed towards the items. "You see it don't you? One of my men was pressed like shit. So after the fool got hit with a rack of shots, we left his punk ass right where he lay. I ain't about to go all into that though. It is what it is. Spider you and your lady friend hold onto one of those 9 mm and fuck it. Maybe yall can do something with the Louis Vuitton bag. I think there's a computer in it. I gotta roll. One of your old partners Pimp LA Smooth opened up one mean ass lounge."

"Oh! Yeah!" I said while I watched him hand the items over to April.

"Yeah! One hell of a place for hustlas and playas to relax. You know Pimp LA Smooth always been up on his game. We are having a serious breakfast.

Y'all take it easy and keep on playing playa.

April handed me the bag and pistol and walked Seven to the back door. When I opened the bag, I thought nothing of it at first. Except when I cut the laptop on, even with a little water damage, I noticed something familiar. The screen saver showed a screen full of money. At the bottom next to Password was an empty box. At that moment April walked back into the room.

"Daddy, you alright?" she asked.

I couldn't answer; I just looked up into her brown eyes and smiled real big.

About the Author

Akil Dorsey Sr. is a proud father and grandfather. He is a leader amongst many whom was born in Washington, DC at Freedmonds Hospital in 1974. Growing up amiss a single parent, Akil spent a numerous amount of time during his life both in and out of the ghettoes that surround the Metropolitan area. He is an educated Author with aspirations of introducing the world to much of his literature and depicts of what many call, "That Life." For some they have never lived that life but Akil and his unfortunate mishaps have made him the man who is able to tell you stories that will make you grip the pages and look forward to what's on the next page.

Contact Akil Dorsey Sr. at
switchinglanesthroughlife@yahoo.com.

Printed in the United States
By Bookmasters